ME + YOU

A COLLEGE ROMANCE

GINA AZZI

Me + You

Copyright © 2019 by Gina Azzi

THE COLLEGE PACT SERIES

Four best friends.
Four sexy athletes.
Four hot romances.
One college pact!

The Last First Game (Lila's Story)
All the While (Maura's Story)
Me + You (Emma's Story)
Kiss Me Goodnight in Rome (Mia's Story)

JULY

PROLOGUE

LUKE

The abandoned firehouse reeks of smoke and weed when I enter, momentarily stinging my eyes and producing a hazy film that envelops everyone in the large space. A demarcated boxing ring waits in the center as hordes of people push and shove around the perimeter.

They're hungry for blood.

Popping my neck from right to left, cracking sounds ripple down my spine.

It's only been two weeks since I've climbed into a ring, but fuck if it doesn't feel like a lifetime.

This is what I'm meant to do; what I need to do.

My fingers twitch with reckless energy, my fists eager to pound on some poor, unassuming bastard.

"Dude, you made it." Gray's mouth twists into a grin, relief shadowing his eyes as he slaps an open palm on my shoulder. "You can get your shit together in the back."

"Yeah." I head in the direction of the grimy bathroom, kicking the door closed behind me. Sweeping the small space, relief fills my chest that it's empty. No one screwing or bumping coke in a bathroom stall. Just a cracked mirror, a leaky faucet, and yellowing subway tiles.

Resting my forehead against the cool glass of the mirror, I close my eyes as adrenaline hums in my veins.

You've got this.

Tonight is one step closer to going pro.

This is who you are.

Win tonight, train tomorrow.

Stay starving.

Uncle Steve's face swims behind my eyelids before I block him out. Getting my head on straight is easy; I live for moments like tonight, for the fight. Besides, if I can make bank tonight, I can clear Gray's debts, settle the bills from Uncle Steve's funeral, and still have money to party away the despair I feel about both.

"Yo! You fucking done yet?" The pounding on the door spurs me into action.

Grabbing tape from my duffle bag, I begin to tape the lower part of my hands and wrists before stopping. "Nothing like bare knuckles." I whisper into the quiet, dropping the tape back into my bag.

Pulling off my hoodie, I glance down at my unassuming black sweats and grey T-shirt. In life, and especially in a fight, it's best to let others underestimate you.

Except no one will underestimate me tonight.

Even four hours from home, I know my reputation precedes me.

Twenty minutes.

In twenty minutes, this will be over.

Done.

Grey's name will be cleared with all the sharks he owes money to.

Uncle Steve will be resting in peace.

And I'll claim one more underground win.

"Yo, you're up," someone yells through the door, knuckles rapping against the splitting wood.

"Coming." Running my mouth guard under the water from the leaky faucet, I give myself one last glance in the mirror. My face is blank, giving nothing away. My shoulders relaxed, my posture casual. No one would guess at the turmoil of rage, the cluster of anger, the need to unleash the fury circling in my stomach, flooding my lungs so I can hardly muster breath.

Twenty minutes.

"What the fuck?" The hand slams at the door again.

A roar erupts when I emerge from the bathroom, a sea of voices that carry my feet all the way to the ring. Shouts of encouragement, curses, threats, phone numbers, all of it assaults my ears. But the moment I step into the ring, I block it all out.

Silence.

My opponent has been in the circuit for a while. He's a regular. Seasoned.

But I note the flicker of uncertainty that licks at his irises when he meets my eyes. He knows me. They all know me. They all know what I'm capable of.

Even two weeks of eating like shit and dropping my training hasn't diminished my ability to step into the ring and own it.

Even burying Uncle Steve and holding Mom upright for the past fourteen days has done nothing to compromise my mental state.

I'm here. I'm starving. And I want this.

The ref goes through a list of rules for show; they're never enforced. Fights like tonight rarely are stopped, even if one of the fighters is on the verge of death. And still, opponents line up for the chance to fight, for a chance to claim the glory.

Money changes hands.

Vodka and tequila glide down open throats.

Smoke burns behind my eyelids.

Fangirls clad in lacy lingerie pose provocatively for self-ies, reeking of desperation, starved for attention.

My opponent stares me down, his brow furrowing.

When the bell rings, I let him throw the first punch as a bone. Circling him, I critique his style. He's overreaching. I allow the round to continue for a full minute for the sake of the crowd. Everyone loves a good show, but I don't have all fucking day. When I decide to stop pulling my punches, I'll end it quickly.

He gets one solid jab in, and then I unleash the anger that eats me whole, raining jabs and crosses on him until my knuckles split and my fists slide off his face, slippery with his blood.

His body crumples to the mat in a heap of limbs, bloody cuts, and swelling bruises.

The crowd hollers and cheers.

Gray pounds my back, yelling in my ear.

Sound returns, clogging out the silence, stealing my few moments of salvation. Of peace.

Money changes hands.

Vodka and tequila glide down open throats.

Fangirls flank me.

"I'm Becca. Let me celebrate with you." One girl in particular pushes her way into my side, curling her arms around my abdomen. I chuckle, wrapping an arm around her shoulder and pulling her closer, ready to mark my victory.

It only took seven minutes.

Losing my fingers in Becca's hair, I tug and plant a sloppy kiss on her mouth. I'm ready to get into some trouble.

I'm ready to put the overwhelming loss and staggering hurt of the past two weeks behind me. For good. For forever.

The Lone Wolf is fucking back.

AUGUST

1

EMMA

"Toss another pancake this way, would ya?" I hold my plate out as Mia spears a pancake with the tines of her fork and holds it as far as humanly possible from her face. It plops down on my plate in a puddle of maple syrup. Delicious. "Girl, you're going to disappear one day if you only subsist on legumes."

Mia blushes as I pour a generous heap of syrup over my pancake. You can never have too much sweet maple goodness, am I right?

"Can you believe today is the day?" Lila squeals, a forkful of scrambled eggs hovering below her chin. "I mean, Mia, you're going to Rome!"

Maura rolls her eyes and coughs into her coffee mug.

Mia looks like she's about to vomit.

Reaching out a hand, I squeeze Mia's cold fingers. "Relax. You're going to be a rock star. This is good for you. For all of us."

"The college pact is everything." Lila adds, earning another eye roll from Maura.

"I love when you speak in superlatives." Maura quips.

Lila ignores her and ticks off the pact criteria on her fingers. "Push past our comfort zones, meet hot guys and date them, be brave and wild, have fun." Lila turns to me, pointing a finger accusingly. "And moving forward. No more being hung up on Josh McCannon."

"Gah! I'm not hung up on him."

Three sets of eyes stare at me, blinking.

"I'm not!"

"Em, Josh McCannon is an idiot. Any guy, any guy Em, would be lucky to date you. And no douchebag, especially not a stupid summer fling with a guy you went to high school with, should ever make you feel bad about yourself. I hate that he made you question your worth. The pact is about embracing everything we are." Lila rants.

Mia nods and even Maura tips her head in agreement.

Big sigh. Josh McCannon. A popular boy from high school whose path crossed with mine at a Memorial Day Weekend party in my home town. We drank too much, flirted a bit, exchanged a very sensual kiss... and continued to hook up for the rest of the summer. It was fun, and carefree, and simple in the way summer hookups are. Everything is of the moment, marking the present with more weight than it should hold in a "fling-type" scenario. It gives a girl ideas that maybe, just maybe, this summer fun could turn into an autumn reality.

And then, two weekends ago, *it* happened. Josh McCannon informed me, not politely either, that it was a fun thing, but he couldn't actually date me. For starters, I look nothing like his "type." Who knew he even had a type? Apparently, he does. His real girlfriend type is more along the lines of tall, blonde, and gorgeous. His real girlfriend type looks like Lila, which seems to be a theme in my life. However, my shorter, stockier build with a layer of chub around the middle and boring brown bangs is a definite hook-up only.

Alas, I digress.

Does it matter?

Probably not.

But after a series of put-downs from a series of guys I liked, the wind has gone out of my sails. I should definitely stop chasing guys that are out of my league. If I want to keep any of my confidence, that is.

"I know, I know." I tell my friends just so they'll stop talking about it. Him. The whole summer.

"I'm serious, Emma."

"So am I, Li."

"I'm going to miss you girls." Mia interjects, pushing her food around her plate.

Me too." I admit, a realization washing over our breakfast table. The four of us have been inseparable since we dormed together in a quad our freshman year at McShain University. We've been through every college milestone together: new relationships, breakups, drunken nights you wish would last forever, hungover mornings you wish you could die, changing majors, family illnesses, family drama, the gamut. But this semester, the start of our senior year, we're all being pulled in new directions for the first time. Ever.

Mia is boarding a plane to study abroad in Rome, Italy. Lila is heading to California to participate in a competitive medical internship program at Astor University. Maura is staying on campus, in Philadelphia, to prepare for her final season as a member of McShain's women's rowing team.

And me, well, I'm about to embark on a dream I've had since the seventh grade. I'm interning on Capitol Hill in Washington, DC, for Senator LeBeau, from my home state, the Small Wonder of Delaware. Although now we're known more for our "Endless Discoveries." I'm still trying to sort that one out...

"Don't forget to update us with emails and FaceTime calls." Lila reminds Mia.

"Promise." Mia runs her fork over her untouched egg white omelet.

"In four months, we'll have the best stories to tell each other, the greatest experiences to share. Get pumped people." Lila raises her mimosa, her blue eyes dancing. "To the College Pact."

"To the College Pact," we echo, clinking our glasses and sharing a smile.

Champagne bubbles tickle my upper lip as I grin at my best friends. Josh McCannon who? This semester is going to be amazing.

SEPTEMBER

2

LUKE

The material of my T-shirt sticks to the center of my back as I place the last box of dishes on the floor. Dragging a hand across my face, I wince as my fingernail snags on the cut underneath my left eye. The salt from my sweat stings.

Leaning my elbows on top of the bar, I hunch forward, my ribs screaming, and take in the disaster around me. The crates of unopened champagne bottles. The boxes full of glasses and plates that need to be washed and stacked away. The pile of placemats, sliding off a dirty table onto the floor. Shit, I need to fix the leg on that table before a customer sits there.

What the hell was I thinking?

What kind of masochist would try to revive and run a restaurant/bar in only two weeks?

Technically, the restaurant is open and running somewhat smoothly, but in two weeks we're going to take it up a notch. Or twelve. Sighing, I close my eyes to recall the long list of things that still need to be bought, fixed, or sorted.

"Hey! You're still here?" Gray walks in through the

kitchen. Dressed in ripped jeans and a V-neck T-shirt, Grayson Harrington is a toss-up between a DC darling and a celebrated playboy. As a poker aficionado, he's a serious gambler who has a penchant for just managing to slip past any consequences. Usually because of me; always trying to keep him out of trouble, I somehow manage to create more for myself.

"Yeah man." I answer him, looking around again at the chaos that surrounds us. "I don't even know where to begin."

"Aw, come on dude, you'll figure it out."

"We live in different realities, Gray."

"I know. I'd never go out in public looking like someone jumped me."

Flipping him my middle finger, he chuckles.

"Where was the fight?" he asks.

"Local."

"Why?"

"Why what?"

"Why are you still fighting? Dude, I appreciate all the shit you did for me after Uncle Steve died. I know I got into some trouble and if you didn't take those fights, I'd be getting my ass handed to me. But you can't fuck around boxing anymore. Uncle Steve left you Barracuda." Gray gestures to the restaurant literally falling down around us. "He trusted you with his legacy. You need to pull yourself together and be an entrepreneur now."

I quirk an eyebrow.

"At least, try and be a respectable business owner."

I tip my head back, pinching the bridge of my nose.

"Tell you what." He smiles cockily, sauntering behind the bar and pouring us each a shot of tequila. "I'll help you out."

"By drinking all the tequila?"

He raises his shot in my direction before tossing it back,

smacking his lips. "By serving it. I'm a natural behind the bar, mixing drinks, charming women, chatting up the political who's who. You know, all the things you suck at."

I take my shot, hissing as the alcohol warms my stomach.

As much as I hate to admit it, Gray has a point. For all his wild ways and ability to avoid consequences for his actions, Gray does have a lot of qualities necessary in the F and B industry. Qualities I lack. Like the polite small talk with customers, the schmoozing required in the DC circle, the general affability of everyone's favorite bartender. He pulls people in with his charisma the same way I push them away with my indifference.

"You're hired."

"Excellent. I'll start tomorrow."

It isn't until later that night, when I'm back home from a grueling workout at the gym, that I allow myself to relax. Collapse on the couch, flip through the channels, a bottle of Corona in my hand. I move my neck from side to side, enjoying the pop and crack that shuffles down my spine as I twist my back. Not used to such long hours of crunching numbers, sorting through stacks of papers, and tracking down permits, my entire body is wound up, too tight. The gym helped some but sparring only clears my mind momentarily. Now that I'm home, the pressure of the debt I'm crumbling under is suffocating once more.

I take a swig of beer, allowing the tangy taste to coat my throat, and lean my head back into the couch cushions. My phone beeps, alerting me to a message.

Uncle Preston: I'm stopping by in ten.

Great. I toss the phone on the coffee table and stack my

feet on top, toeing off my sneakers and letting them fall onto the table as well.

What the hell could Uncle Preston want to speak with me about now?

I run through our agreement in my mind, mentally assessing any loopholes I may be missing. Coming up blank, I turn off the TV and stand, gathering my sneakers and random articles of clothing and tossing them into the hall closet just as a knock sounds on the door.

Pulling it open, I come face to face with Uncle Preston. He's dressed impeccably, looking every bit the Senator. A crisp white shirt even though he's been at the office since 7:00AM, a perfectly tailored navy suit, red tie. His jacket is folded expertly over his arm and a cell phone is clutched in his hand. Uncle Preston's blue eyes are cool and assessing. Calculating. For as much as he resembles my father in looks, one glance at his eyes notifies you that he's nothing like the man Theodore Harrington was.

"Hey Uncle P. Come on in." I push the door open wider for him, holding up my beer. "Want one?"

A flash of disgust crosses his face before he masks it. "No thank you, Lucas. Just need to have a few words is all." He walks into my apartment, scanning the space. There's not much to see: a sectional from Ikea, a beat-up coffee table I purchased off Craigslist, a modest but clean kitchen, and an open door indicating my bedroom at the back. All my worldly possessions.

"Well, I can see that you must have really needed the money."

I nod once, not trusting my voice to speak. I didn't need the money because I want to live like some flashy playboy and party in the nation's capital, and he knows it. After sinking most of my savings into Uncle Steve's medical care, spending the money I won from a series of fights on Gray's debts and Uncle Steve's funeral, I'm pretty much broke. He's purposely trying to push my buttons. Knowing this, I clamp my mouth shut, clenching my teeth.

When I drove up to Connecticut to ask Uncle Preston for a loan, he said I should just sell Barracuda, take the money, and get on with my life. Part of me wonders if he's right. I mean, on some level I'm sure he is. The smart, business, logical level. But I couldn't do that to Uncle Steve, not after he entrusted me with something so precious. Not after he stepped into the father role I desperately needed when my own passed. And I can't do that to Mom. She needs this.

Fighting for the funds crossed my mind, but I didn't have enough time to pull it all together before losing the loan to the bank. So, I went groveling. All the way to Uncle P's massive estate in Connecticut. And he agreed to help me out.

With conditions.

Conditions that make my fingers curl into fists.

"Any progress with Grayson?" He raises his eyebrows.

"I don't know what you expect, Uncle P. Gray's always done things his own way. He'll make up his own mind about how to support your campaign announcement and if he wants to be a part of it."

Uncle P sighs, rubbing the space between his eyebrows. "I need him on board with this. It will help me immensely if he would take his rightful place by my side." He cuts me a look, eyeing my sweats. "And if you would quit acting like Rocky Balboa and groom yourself into a respectable business owner."

I nod even though I couldn't disagree more. Uncle P trying to push Gray into a political career is absurd. Uncle P is a senator. Elected by the American people. Not some oil tycoon trying to pass his company off onto his offspring.

Gray has never shown an active interest in politics, but man, does Uncle P push. Especially now that he wants to make a run for the Republican Presidential nomination. I wonder if he would push so hard if he knew the truth about Gray's gambling, the mountains of debt he's hidden over the years, the scrapes I've pulled him out of with my fists.

"I need both of you on board with this."

"What?" Confusion rocks through me. *What could Uncle P want with me?*

"Lucas, you and my son are practically brothers. What will the media think when they see Grayson supporting me but not you?"

I shrug, waiting for him to explain. I don't give a fuck about what the media will think. Or anyone else for that matter.

"You need to be seen supporting me like a father figure."

My fingers begin to tremble with an inferno that sweeps my bloodstream at Uncle P's words. A father figure? Is he delusional? He practically cast Mom and me to the wolves after Dad died. Uncle Steve was my father figure while Uncle P was the devil incarnate.

Loan, loan, loan.

Grasping onto the word, I temper my anger and bite out, "I'm not interested in politics." My stomach churns and I feel sick.

"I don't know why you make your life harder, Lucas. You and Grayson stand beside me, do the right thing, and forget the loan, the money's yours. But you always have to fight, always have to prove something. You borrowed a lot of money from me, Lucas, why not take the easier out?"

Because I'm not you. "I'll pay you back, Uncle P."

"You're call," he sneers, clapping me on the shoulder. "But I'm announcing my bid in March, so I at least need

Grayson on board by January. Four months from now. Otherwise, I'll need that loan back. With interest."

"Thanks for stopping by."

"Goodnight, Lucas. Get some sleep, you look ragged," he says in farewell, his polished shoes clapping against the floor as he exits my apartment, closing the door behind him.

I stand still for several moments, waiting until I hear the ding from the elevator before I collapse back onto the couch and take another swig of my Corona.

Somehow, it tastes less tangy, and more like rust.

3

EMMA

The Capitol Building.

Rising before me, straight pillars and a gleaming white dome, the presence of the building is overwhelming. I'm reminded of all the incredible, intelligent, determined men and women who walked these stairs before me. Here, our country's seat of power, the history of our nation has unfolded. And now, I'm going to be a part of that history. In a tiny fingerprint kind of way but still, I'm here.

Adjusting the long strap of my sleek black purse and straightening the seams on my pencil skirt, I start to walk the stairs when my phone rings.

"Dad?"

"Is this the girl who's going to be our first female president in 2024? Or is it 2028?"

"Don't get ahead of yourself, Daddy. I haven't even started my internship yet."

"Late on the first day?"

I laugh, rolling my eyes. "Interrupted is more like it."

"I was just calling to wish you luck, Em."

"Thanks Dad."

"And hey, quick question."

"What's up?" I run the toe of my black pump along the edge of the stair.

"Did you activate your new MasterCard yet?"

"Uh, no."

"Okay, well maybe you could hold off on that for a bit."

"Yeah, sure. Is everything okay, Dad?"

"Of course, sweetheart. You know, sometimes it's just a lot with the four of you and three in college."

"Yeah." He's right. It is a lot. But still, asking me about a credit card is something my Dad has never done. "Well, no worries, I don't even need the card."

"Really?" He sounds hopeful and my stomach sinks. Suddenly, the giddiness I was feeling about my first day sours.

"Yeah, it's fine. I have enough savings for the semester so I'm good." *Such a lie.*

"Oh. Well, that's great. Thanks, Emmy."

"Uh-huh."

"Well, I've got to jump on a conference call. Just wanted to wish you luck on your first day. Enjoy it and enjoy drinks with your roommate later. Just be careful."

"I will. Love you, Daddy."

"Love you too, Emmy girl."

He ends the call and I drop my phone back into my purse. So strange. Dad has never cared about my spending habits before. He must be getting really stressed with Jon starting college too. But jeez, what was I even thinking saying I didn't need the credit card? I barely have a savings… and, shoot, I'm going to be late on my first day.

Trying to block Dad's call from my mind, I square my shoulders and face my future.

Stepping inside the Capitol Building, I wait in line to pass the necessary metal detectors and security checks. Once I'm cleared I head to Senator LeBeau's office, where I am immediately greeted by one of his staffers, Zoe.

"Good morning. I'm Emma." I introduce myself.

"Glad to have you with us this semester. Want to take a seat here and I'll go over some of the tasks you'll be responsible for?"

"Sure." I sit on the sofa and pull out a notepad and pen. Perching on the edge of the couch, I'm like a baby bird about to fall from the nest.

"I know the first day can be overwhelming, but it's still pretty cool to be here, huh?"

"Am I that obvious?"

"Yeah. Don't worry, the other intern, Courtney, was the exact same when she started last week."

I laugh.

Zoe grins. "I was the same on my first day too. In fact, it's easy to spot all the interns that descend on DC over the summer and the first week of September and end of January. Y'all have that bright-eyed gleam and eager jump in your step."

"I definitely have that."

"Everyone does when they start out. Now, I want to go over what you'll be doing during your time here. I'll introduce you to people as they come in and out of the office and get you settled working with Courtney. You'll meet Senator LeBeau sometime today too."

"Okay."

"Great." She leans forward and begins to outline what a typical day will look like for me over the next four months.

I hang on to every word, occasionally taking notes, gratitude for the privilege of working on The Hill mounting with every minute. Even the unglamorous nature of the tasks doesn't affect my enthusiasm for this opportunity.

Basically, I'll be a gofer, doing things like answering phones, taking messages, guiding tours for constituents from Delaware, preparing the office for the day by sorting the mail and listening to the voicemail messages in the morning, and of course, ensuring that everyone who needs caffeine receives it.

"Come on, I'll introduce you to Jenn, Senator LeBeau's Chief of Staff, as well as the LD and LA's. And once Courtney is back from the tour she is shadowing, you'll meet her too."

The rest of the day passes in a blur of names and information. By 5:00 PM, strolling back to the metro stop, my head is spinning with all the issues I can't wait to research. Super excited to go home and Google a ton of topics, my phone beeps with a message from my new roommate, Cassie.

Cassie: Hey girl, finished for the day?

Me: Hi! Yes, just walking to the metro.

Cassie: Sweet. Happy hour drinks at Leapy Frogs in Dupont Circle? 5:30PM?

Me: Done! Can't wait to meet you.

Cassie: Same. We need tequila and nachos.

Me: Tequila? We're going to be besties by dinner!

Eek! How exciting is it all?

I'm such a real person in DC!

Except that after Dad's phone call this morning, it's clear I need to find another job...one that pays.

THE EASTERN MARKET IN DC has its own vibe.

A bit eclectic with homemade crafts and local, fresh food, the area boasts a handful of awesome restaurants and eateries, close to Capitol Hill. It's here that I begin my search for a server position. Sure, I'm not technically qualified in the food and beverage industry, but I'm bubbly, personable, and can concoct a mean Bloody Mary or vodka cranberry when necessary.

For my first three years at McShain University, it never crossed my mind to find a side gig for some spending money. Dad sent me a monthly allowance and I learned to manage those funds, only going over once or twice, or maybe five or six times, in all my college career.

But now, with Dad's call about the credit card, I've been reevaluating things. Daphne and Jon are both in college and Celia is a junior in high school. As such, it seems only fair that a considerable portion of my spending money has been redistributed. Plus, I've noticed other things. Like how he downgraded his car last year, cancelled one of his two gym memberships, and didn't even mention his and Mom's annual trip to Hawaii this summer.

So, as the eldest, I've decided to help out. At least, to do what I can.

And I'm sure I can be a server. I mean, how hard can it be, right?

APPARENTLY, harder than I thought. I must be the only college-aged kid in the city who has never held a hostess, server, or bartender position before. I'm nearing the end of Eighth Street and I've already been rejected by nine restaurants and coffee houses. Steeling my shoulders for lucky number ten, I slide my sweaty palms down the sides of my hips, smoothing out a wrinkle in my tunic.

Walking into the brightly colored Cajun restaurant, I smile at the guy behind the bar and ask to speak to the manager.

"Sure thing." He nods, tossing a bar towel over his left shoulder. His biceps bunch as he leans forward, bracing his arms against the bar. "You here to fill out an application?"

"Yes. But I'd really like to speak with the manager or whoever does the hiring, if that's possible." Let's be real, I suck on paper. I have zero experience. My only hope here is charming the hiring manager or owner or whoever with my winning smile and fantastic personality. I need face time.

"Luke!" The hottie behind the bar calls out.

"What's up?" a guy strolls out of a back office.

And woah.

My jaw drops open and I remind myself to close my mouth and breathe. Not the large, gulps of breath my stuttering heart is demanding, but normal breathing. You know, where I don't look like a pucker fish.

Because Luke is…everything. More than hot, he's beautiful. Strong, muscled arms and broad shoulders clad in a black T-shirt. Worn, ripped jeans hang low on his hips and hug his thighs. His hair is dark, tousled, as if he just rolled out of bed or ran his fingers through it in thought. Full lips, a well-defined jaw, and sweeping cheekbones give him a touch of classical beauty enshrined in the rugged body of a very modern man. Ink scrawls down his arms, patches of brightly colored images surrounded by black script and bold print. Even his knuckles are tatted.

My breath catches in my throat and I work to swallow. I begin to step forward, extending my hand to introduce myself.

Just then, his gaze cuts to me and I falter, my outstretched hand dropping to my side.

His eyes are a deep green. So deep, I get lost in them for a moment and time seems to stop. And if that's not cliché, I don't know what is. But there you have it.

"She's here about an application," the bartender fills in, pulling me back to the present and reminding me that I'm here for a job, not a date with the boss.

"Hi." I extend my hand again. "I'm Emma."

He takes my hand in his, offering a firm squeeze and shake. A surge of excitement jolts up my arm, making my fingertips tingle. "Good to meet you." He lets go, crossing his arms over his chest and leaning his hip against a table. "You looking for a job?"

I nod, steadying my breath. Reaching into my purse to extract my resume I fiddle with the buckle instead, deciding to try an alternative approach. I mean, I've already been turned down nine times. *What do I have to lose at this point?*

"Yes. My name is Emma Stanton. I just moved to DC for the semester for an internship on Capitol Hill. My hours are nine to five but after that, my schedule is flexible. I don't have any formal experience serving but I can assure you that I'm very friendly, punctual, hardworking, and a fast learner. Plus, I really need this job." I grin. "So I'm willing to do whatever it takes for employment." I cringe slightly, mentally face-palming myself. *No need to sound like a prostitute, Emma.* "Any positions you have available, hostess, bussing, serving, whatever, I'd like to be considered for."

Behind the bar, the hottie busies himself cleaning glasses, looking up every now and then to assess the conversation between Luke and me.

Luke studies me carefully, his face giving nothing away. He tilts his head to the left as his eyes watch me for several moments, just enough time to become uncomfortable before he clears his throat. "You willing to do a three-day trial?"

"Of course."

"Alright. Well, I'll see if Anna can come in this week to train you and –"

"I can train her," Bartender Hottie speaks up, causing both Luke and I to stare at him.

"Gray, you've got a lot going on and I don't want to dump this on you. If Anna –"

"Anna just started her master's program at George Mason. If anything, she wants to cut back on her hours. It's no problem." Gray interjects, grinning at me. "In fact, I think it'd be pretty fun. Don't you, Emma?" His eyes dare me, a deep brown with hints of black.

"Uh, sure."

"Then it's settled." Gray leans forward on the bar, turning his full stare toward Luke. "If it's all good with you, Luke?"

Luke nods, one snap of his neck. "Gray will be here to meet you tomorrow at 5:30PM. Wear black pants, jeans are fine, and a black T-shirt. An apron will be provided. Don't be late."

"Thank you so much." I gush at Luke. "I promise I'll work really hard and be a great employee. You won't regret it."

The left side of Luke's mouth ticks up in an almost smile but he doesn't say anything.

"Oh, I don't doubt it," Gray throws in, smiling at me wickedly.

I blush as I lift my hand in his direction. "See you tomorrow."

"Five-thirty," Luke reminds me.

"I'll be waiting." Gray sings.

The door to the restaurant closes behind me and I hustle around the corner before leaning against the nearest building, my breaths coming out in short bursts.

How the hell am I supposed to work with two of the hottest men I've ever seen?

4

LUKE

"I'm just saying, she's got a great ass."

"Don't get any ideas." I glare at Gray, already noting how his eyes gleam with the prospect of a challenge. I know Gray. If I deem Emma off limits, it will only add to his intention to claim her. If for no other reason than to show me he can.

Sighing, I walk over to the bar and lean my elbows on top, hunching forward.

"Now you want a drink?"

"Nah, too many coffees already today. I feel fucking jittery from all the caffeine."

"Stop overthinking everything, man. It's going to be fine. At least you have another person to add to your payroll."

I snort. Payroll. Not something I can cut out of the budget.

"Here." Gray passes me a Corona with a lime wedged in the top of the bottle. "I can't watch this anymore." He gestures toward me. "You're bringing me down."

I take a swig of the beer. "Yeah, I can imagine how hard all of this is for you."

"Dude, you've got to chill. Stop looking at this," he gestures his hand in a circle, encompassing the restaurant, "as some sort of shit deal you got stuck with, and start viewing it as an opportunity. You can turn this place into a gold mine. At the same time, it will give your mom some peace and probably make that dark soul of yours a few shades lighter knowing you're doing something good in your uncle's memory. This is an opportunity, not a jail sentence."

I close my eyes. He's right. Deep down I know he's right, but I can't stop thinking of every single thing that can go wrong, about all the people, even the dead ones, counting on me to make this right. I can't stop obsessing about my dream to box professionally, as it seems to float further from reality with each day I spend flipping through financial statements and checking inventory instead of training.

I need to tackle each issue with Barracuda one day at a time. I need to get to opening night and then reassess if Barracuda has any chance of succeeding.

"You're right." I tell Gray instead of unloading all the worries taking up space in my mind.

"Of course I'm right," he agrees, pouring himself another cocktail.

IT's LATE when the metal door to The Cellar clicks shut behind me.

Cliff looks up from behind the desk, "Thought you were skipping today."

"Nah, man. Just got a little tied up is all."

"That's good," he glances back at his paperwork.

It's a strange comment from Cliff. No one here tracks my schedule or anything. I mean, I'm in training for my eventual shot to turn my passion into a professional career, but I'm not in training for a specific fight.

Dropping my bag in the corner of the gym, I survey who's here, who's working on what. That's what I love about The Cellar. It's small, quiet, almost intimate. The guys who are here want to be here. There's no drama, no bullshit. Everyone checks their hang-ups at the door and when you're in here, you're here to work. It's an unwritten code that everyone follows.

Wrapping my hands, I start on the speed bag and work my way over to lifting and skipping rope.

"You're here." Toby comes up behind me so quietly, I jump.

"Yeah, man."

"Good. Spar with Manny."

"Huh?" I start to turn in his direction, but he ducks down and pretends to rummage in my bag for something. "Why would I spar with Manny?"

"Just trust me." He stands up, tosses me my gloves, and lopes away.

Turning back to the gym, I spot Manny hanging over the ropes of the ring. He grins at me and his eyes glint with something I can't place. He's... excited. As if something is about to go down.

That's when I hear the voices and see them; Frankie, the owner, and a guy who's reputation precedes him, Scoop. Scoop "Hurricane" Rayes was a top heavyweight contender throughout the late eighties before he claimed the championship belt in the early nineties. He held it for years, as unstoppable as a hurricane. Everyone wants to train under him, learn from him, call him 'coach'. *What the hell is he doing here? Why is he chatting up Frankie?*

"Let's go," Manny calls out, flipping his chin in my direction.

Clearing my head from the distracting tangents my mind is running wild with, I slip on my gloves, and climb into the ring. Manny gives me a few minutes to warm up while Toby tosses me my mouth guard and a bottle of water.

"You ready for me?" Manny asks in that mocking tone of his. He's got a smaller build than me, but man, can he pack a punch. He's all muscle, not an ounce of body fat, and nearly a decade younger than I am.

Still, he doesn't stand a chance and he knows it.

"Give me your best."

He blows me a kiss and I pretend to catch it and slap it against my heart.

"Stop with the fucking antics," Toby hisses next to the ring.

Manny rolls his eyes as I smirk.

But when Toby starts the timer, all joking disappears. It's just the ring, the fighter across from me, and the moment. I block out the noise. I forget every shitty thing that happened today.

Everything disappears except the heavy gaze of Scoop "Hurricane" Rayes that settles between my shoulder blades. And stays there even after the bell dings.

5 :27 PM.

Thank God I'm not late.

Another first day, a new set of nerves.

"On time and everything," Gray leans across the bar, a towel tossed over his left shoulder.

"Aiming to please on my first day. I just need to change." I glance down at the pencil skirt and silk blouse I wore to my internship this morning.

"By all means." Gray tosses me a short black apron. "The bathroom is over there, to the left. Want something to drink?"

"A Diet Coke would be great." Making my way to the bathroom, I take a deep breath and pull out the black jeans, black tee, and an old pair of black Guess sneakers Daphne must have snuck into my suitcase. Dressing quickly, I lace up my sneakers and tie the apron around my waist. A quick assessment in the mirror has me pulling my hair into a low ponytail and pinching my cheeks for extra color. I think this is as good as it's gonna get.

Back at the bar, I take a long sip of the Diet Coke Gray poured. God, I miss Seven Eleven Big Gulps.

"Okay, let's get started."

I place the soda down. "Sounds good."

Over the next several hours, Gray manages all the tables that come in, with me as his shadow. He gives me a tour of the restaurant, introduces me to the other staff members, all of whom work in the kitchen, and runs me through the food and drink menus. I learn how to roll silverware, where the salt, pepper, ketchup, and vinegar are stored for refills, and even make my first martini.

Gray blanches when he tries it, a shaky smile on his lips. "We'll work on that."

I laugh.

All in all, training isn't terrible and I'm surprised when 9:00PM rolls around and Luke strolls in the front door.

He stops suddenly when his eyes slam into mine, a flicker of something, maybe regret, in his irises. "Hey."

"Luke," Gray nods.

"How'd she do?" he asks over my head.

I open my mouth to defend myself but snap it shut as nerves ricochet in my chest.

How did I do?

"She's great," Gray says easily, like it's the truth. "Customers will love her. She's a fast learner and has the personality for this type of thing."

Luke nods once in his curt, businesslike fashion. "Hungry?"

"Come on, newbie. You've got the seal of approval. Now, we eat." Gray nudges the small of my back and I shuffle forward.

But not before I note how Luke zeros in on the gesture, his eyes narrowing, his mouth thinning.

"You can order whatever you like." Gray drops his hand as we enter the kitchen.

The breath I didn't realize I was holding leaves my lips as a sense of relief mixed with pride swells in my chest. I have a job. And I earned it all on my own. It's somehow more than just landing the internship at my dad's old college buddy, Senator LeBeau's, office.

"I'll need you to come in on Mondays, Tuesdays, and Thursdays at 5:30 PM. Plus the occasional weekend brunch at 8:00 AM." Luke's voice, hard and gruff, like gravel mixed with sand, stops me.

Turning, I note his rounded shoulders, the way he's hunched over the bar, his forearms holding him up, almost as if he's in pain. He looks utterly exhausted. Still, a glint of steel rings his irises, his gaze never leaving my face.

"Does this mean I have the job? I can still do the other two days of training." *Stop talking, Emma. The man is giving you an opportunity and you're making him question his decision to hire you.*

He blinks, and I'm rendered speechless by the emotion that fills his eyes. Dark and stormy, like the blue-green water of the Caribbean before a hurricane, a violent mixture of frustration, pain, and... vulnerability.

I swallow.

He drops his head, cutting off my glimpse of his anguish. "No need. You're hired. You'll be great." He says it quietly, almost like he's admitting it to himself.

I still at his words, trying to understand his tone. "Thank you." I mutter as Gray drops the swinging door closed.

"Senator LeBeau's office, Emma speaking, how may I direct your call?"

The woman on the line asks for information regarding

tours of the Capitol and I exhale, rattling off the necessary information before placing the receiver down.

A burst of laughter behind me has me cutting my head to the left. My mouth drops open in shock as Gray stands in the doorway of the office. Gray from the bar. Gray who is training me in my other job. The one that provides a paycheck.

"Gray!"

"Don't act so surprised, Stanton. Isn't that one of the first tips of living in DC? You never really know who anyone is, or who they're connected to." His eyes shine with amusement as he collapses on one of the sofas just inside the entrance and crosses an ankle over his other knee, his foot jangling. "So, this is where you spend your days?"

"What are you doing here?"

"Relax, I was in the building and heard your voice through the open door. Thought I'd pop in and annoy you."

"Just in the building, were you?"

He chuckles. "My dad has the office next door."

What?

My mouth drops open again.

"You need to work on your poker face or this town will eat you alive."

"Your dad? Your dad is Senator Harrington?"

"Correct."

Senator Harrington. Staunch Republican, conservative to the core, a real hard-ass on all issues pertaining to immigration. And refugees. And women's healthcare. And pretty much everything I care about.

And yet, he raised Gray. *How weird is that?* Over the past ten days of my training, Gray and I have become friendly. We joke around, talk, and I listen as Gray tells me all about his relationship woes. Trust me, there are a lot of them. Mainly because there are a lot of women involved.

"I never would have guessed."

"I know. It's because I got all the looks in my family." He bats his eyelashes and I chuck a pen at his head.

"Keep dreaming."

He catches the pen easily and slides it into the pocket of his dress shirt, looking like a complete nerd. Albeit a hot nerd. "Thanks for the pen."

"Grayson! I thought that was you." Senator LeBeau smiles as he strides into the office, holding out his hand to Gray.

Gray hops up, shaking the senator's hand. "How's it going, Senator?"

"Very well, thanks. Are you here to have lunch with your old man?"

"Yes, sir. Just thought I'd annoy your intern first."

My skin grows hot and sticky under the attention of both men.

Please don't say anything dumb, Gray. My entire future is riding on this internship. I need to perform spectacularly and leave DC with a real, paying job lined up for after graduation.

"Ah, you know Emma?" LeBeau offers me a wink. "Go easy on her, Grayson, she's a solid addition to my team. The Hill needs more people like her."

My cheeks blush brighter at the senator's compliment as I smile awkwardly, hoping my face reflects the sweet pink of a sunrise and not the glaring red of a sunburn.

"I'm sure. She's a very hard worker. Well, sir, I better go round up my father. Great seeing you." He shakes the Senator's hand again and picks up a Werther's Original from the candy dish on the end table next to a hideous lamp. "Now you know why I really popped in, Stanton." He quips over his shoulder, unwrapping the candy and popping it into his mouth.

LeBeau chuckles as I fight the urge to sag in relief or stick my tongue out at Gray's back for being so annoying. "'Bye, Gray."

He waves over his shoulder, walking out the door and turning left toward his dad's office.

"AH, THERE SHE IS." Gray grins at me from behind the bar.

"Don't you have a real job?" I scoff, earning a laugh from Luke who pops his head up from behind the bar.

"Hey, Emma."

"Hi, Luke."

Gray narrows his eyes at me. I wait until Luke disappears behind the bar again before sticking my tongue out at him. He chuckles, amused.

"You really are a child," he says to me.

"I have no idea what you're talking about."

"Sure, sure." He grabs a glass from behind the bar, filling it with ice and Diet Coke. After popping in a lemon slice, he pushes it in my direction.

"How was lunch with your dad?"

"Lunch was good."

"You saw Uncle Preston today?" Luke's head snaps back up, a dirty bar rag clenched in his fist.

Gray nods, cutting a quick look in my direction.

Shoot, was that a secret?

"How's he doing?" Luke presses.

"Good, dude. You know, the usual."

Luke slaps his hand against the edge of the bar. "Okay. Well, I've got a few errands to run. See you guys in a bit."

"Later, dude."

"'Bye, Luke."

Luke smiles at me as he passes, his face transforming from a block of marble to a ray of sunshine. I suck in a breath, surprised at how beautiful he is when he isn't scowling.

A moment later, he's gone.

"Crushing on the boss man, are you?"

"I wasn't. I'm not."

Gray snorts, laughing as he takes a swig of beer. "Whatever you say, Stanton. We'll work on that poker face yet."

6

EMMA

I'm in the weeds.

Friday night at Barracuda is packed, groups of people huddling around the bar, every table occupied, the patio at capacity.

"We're getting paid tonight, Stanton."

"Didn't think you needed to work for tips, Gray."

He snorts, his eyes darkening. "We all have our vices, Emma."

"You're right. I'm sorry." I balance a tray of Hurricanes and offer a sheepish grin. "I'm glad we're getting paid."

"You and me both."

As the kitchen becomes swamped with orders, Luke hurries through the front door, his eyes wide with surprise at the number of occupied tables in the restaurant. This is clearly an all-hands-on-deck moment and he wastes no time joining Gray behind the bar to mix cocktails and punch in orders.

Taking a deep breath, I survey the fifteen tables I'm running. *Way out of your league here, Emma.* Still, the energy in Barracuda is pulsing and I can sense that tonight is a big night; an important moment for Luke, Gray, the bar, myself.

Steeling my shoulders, I paste a smile on my lips and spend the next three hours in a whirlwind of activity. Forgoing water, skipping dinner, and staying on my hustle, a throbbing sensation settles in my spine, vibrating up my back from all the trays I've lifted over my head tonight.

The kitchen is bumping, regatton playing from an old CD player, clipped Spanish and bursts of laughter ringing out in between the rhythmic staccato of knives hitting the chopping blocks, spatulas tossing fried peppers and onions, and plates sliding between the hands of Jorge, Raoul, and Hector.

The buzz from the dining area keeps the guys moving at a steady pace, their obvious comfort around each other minimizing errors and ensuring an efficient working environment.

"You holding up out there, Chica?" Jorge asks, plating a heaping serving of Cajun chicken linguine.

Waving a hand over my shoulder, I smirk. "I used to organize Cliff Hill High's annual prom dress drive; this is nothing." I glance at the ticket orders to make sure I'm loading my tray with table seven's order.

Raoul chuckles, whistling between his teeth. "It hasn't been like this in ages, girl. Tonight, shit's lit! We're gonna celebrate."

Hector snorts, coming around the metal divider to pull me into his arms and twirl me around the kitchen. "Don't worry, Pequena, you're doing a damn good job." He kisses the back of my hand before adding a side of jambalaya to my tray. "Table seven's good."

Laughing at their antics, my chest fills with relief and gratitude for their encouragement. I heave the tray up onto my right shoulder, keeping my right hand flat and center to balance the weight, like Raoul showed me, as I bound through the double doors and head straight to table seven.

You can do this, Emma.

By midnight, the rush has died down and the crowd trickles out. I finally have a moment to breathe a huge sigh of relief and pop into the bathroom to lean my head against the door and thank all that is holy for letting me survive the crazy chaos. Checking my reflection in the mirror, I can't stop the smile that splits my face. Sure, my hair is a literal disaster, my bangs separated in the center and moving in different directions, strands of hair plastered to the base of my neck and tucked errantly behind my ears. But my cheeks are flushed, my eyes glowing, and I look happy for someone who spent an entire Friday night of their twenty-first year running around a hot kitchen and dining room like a chicken without its head. But I did it on my own and for some reason, that validation settles deep in my stomach and causes my smile to blossom into an actual laugh. I shake my head, my fingers sweeping over my bangs and tugging on my hair to tighten my ponytail. Tonight was like nothing I'd ever experienced before.

Leaving the bathroom behind, I'm surprised that the last of the patrons is closing out their tabs and talking animatedly with Gray before leaving the restaurant, their hands lifted in farewell.

After the door closes behind them, Luke hurries over and flicks the lock. He leans his back against the door and taps his head against the wood, his eyes closing, shoulders sagging.

"That was some way to kick start your re-opening weekend, Luke!" Gray whoops.

Luke nods, his eyes fluttering open. His gaze connects with mine and I suck in an inhale. A mixture of relief, pride, and a touch of sadness swims in their deep green depths before he blinks, his expression impassive once more. "You were great tonight."

"Thanks."

"But we all know I was the real superstar," Gray announces, grabbing a stack of shot glasses and a bottle of tequila. "I need a drink. Hey, Amigos! Get your asses out here and come drink with us," he yells toward the kitchen.

Laughing at the absurdity of the last several hours, I collapse on the barstool, suddenly very aware of how sore I am, how tired my body feels, how happy I am to just sit. "Thanks, Gray." I pick up a shot of Patron. Once Luke and the guys from the kitchen gather around, a meaningful pause settles over our huddle.

"Thank you guys, really, for making tonight so successful. I had no idea what to expect, maybe a shit ton of disasters, but it definitely wasn't this." Luke chuckles after a beat, but it lacks humor. "Cheers."

"Cheers!" the rest of us echo, holding up our glasses.

Gray inclines his head toward Luke who nods, a sad smile spreading across his lips.

"To Uncle Steve," Luke whispers.

"To Steve," everyone murmurs solemnly.

I look down at my shot glass and observe the natural silence that follows. Once Gray tosses back his shot, I do the same, wincing as the clear liquid hits the back of my throat.

Luke stands before me, holding a lime that I bite into, surprising us both.

His eyes spark before darkening dangerously, a rawness raking over his features. His cheekbones sharpen, his jaw tightens, and a low growl sounds in the back of his throat. He doesn't blink as he shifts closer, my thighs widening as he steps between my legs. Awareness spikes low in my stomach, my veins humming with adrenaline. And desire. Definitely desire.

The rough pads of Luke's fingers brush across my lips as he removes the lime from my mouth, his hand hovering in the air. His knuckles slip down the curve of my neck, his ink bleeding into my skin, pressing secrets I don't understand into my bloodstream. My skin blazes hot under his touch, as I lean closer, desperate for ... what?

"Thank you, Emma. For everything." His voice is low, a hum of vibrations that I barely make out but feel throughout my body, filling up places I didn't know were empty. Because as he gazes down at me, the scent of lime engulfing us, his expression softens.

And I see *him*.

The desperate, broken man behind the façade.

And he's so damn beautiful, I'm forced to blink.

7

LUKE

"Trying to close with Emma?"

"What?" *Did Gray catch that? Shit, the last thing I need is for him to get some wild idea about Emma and me. Because there is no Emma and me. Never will be.*

"Dude, you're into Stanton. Don't bullshit me."

I shake my head, easily sliding out of Gray's headlock and moving a few paces away. A chill hangs in the night air, hinting at winter. Crossing over Eighth Street, we turn up Independence Avenue and I can feel Gray's eyes on me, searching for confirmation that there is something between Emma and me. *Jesus, I need to shut this down before his imagination goes off the grid.*

"She's a nice girl, a good girl. She did real good tonight, too." Tonight, Barracuda reopened in a way that so much bigger than I ever imagined. Every table occupied, a constant rotation of customers, Uncle Steve's dream turned into reality. The bar was packed with staffers from the Hill, employees from various NGO's, the GW grad school crowd. It was exactly as Uncle Steve hoped it would be: a meeting place for anyone and everyone to enjoy good food, strong drinks, and interesting conversations. He would have been proud.

But afterwards, shit. I got caught up in the moment. In the relief that finally, something went right, the way I intended it to. And looking at Emma, exhaustion marring her features while she smiled at me, as if she understood, as if *she* was proud, Jesus, I wanted to reach out and trace the curve of her lips. Palm her cheeks and dig my fingers into her hair. Tug her lower lip between my teeth. Wrap her up and take her home like my own personal present, unwrapping her slowly.

Impossible.

Never going to happen.

I'm not the right guy for her. The girls that are into me are nothing like Emma. They smoke cigarettes and drink whisky from the bottle. They prance around in skimpy clothes, one size too small, leaving nothing to the imagination. They want bragging rights in some warped, convoluted circle of ex-felons and fangirls.

"She's a great girl. That's good, isn't it?" Gray prods, poking at a sore spot he knows he shouldn't.

"It's a great thing, if you're a good guy."

"You're right. I forgot what a shit person you are. I mean, you're a real bastard for keeping your uncle's restaurant going just so his dream would live on and it would give your mom some peace of mind. Only a dick would do that."

"Fuck off, Gray."

He holds his hands up in mock surrender. "All I'm saying, dude, is that there are sparks there. And yeah, she's a good girl. So what? You can only screw sluts with a social agenda? That's discrimination, you know?"

Sometimes I want to punch Gray in the face and knock him out. This is one of those times. "She deserves more. Better."

"Well Jesus, Luke, you don't have to put a ring on her finger."

"Eventually, I want to box, Gray. You know that."

"So?"

"Right now, my only focus is the restaurant. I've got to get this up and running. I've got to grow this business. It's got to be successful."

"So you can't date because you're someone with a business? You're right. Entrepreneurs definitely don't date."

"But afterwards, I'm going to box. Professionally."

"Good for you."

"Jesus, what don't you get? I can't be with a girl like Emma. It's not fair."

"To who?"

I pinch the bridge of my nose so hard I swear the bone creaks. "To her."

Gray smiles that annoying grin, looking carefree as ever. "So you do like her then."

"Gray." I pause, unsure of how much I want to reveal to him. "She's different. A woman like her can have any future she wants. She's got her own expectations of what that future looks like. Trust me, it doesn't include a guy like me. And yeah, I'd love to take her home, toss her in my bed, and keep her underneath me for a week. But she's not the type of woman who does casual; she's not some random fangirl out for a good time. Emma is more than that and I won't treat her as less. Yeah?"

Gray clears his throat, his expression so serious, it's solemn. "Yeah."

I WANT to bang my head against a wall.

Literally.

This morning, I want to knock myself out.

You ever have one of those mornings when you know, the moment you open your eyes, before you even have a cup of shit coffee, that everything is going to go to shit? Yep. I knew it the second I rolled over and heard the pinging of raindrops against my bedroom window. *What is it about rain that casts a gloom over everything?*

Anyway, I got up because I had to. Made my shit cup of coffee. And picked up my phone to scroll through my messages and emails. That's when I saw it.

Anna (2:43AM): Hey Luke, I won't be able to come in today for my shift. Sorry.

Anna (3:13AM): Hi. I'm so sorry to do this to you but I have to leave town unexpectedly. Family emergency. I'm not sure when I'll be back. Let me know when you get this. Again, so sorry.

Anna (5:27AM): Luke? Did you get my messages? Please give me a call. I can try and find some friends to cover for me.

Even though I'm annoyed at what this means for Barracuda, my immediate concern is Anna. *Is her family okay? Is it even a family emergency or something else? Trouble with a guy?* My skin crawls at the thought.

I call her, but her phone goes straight to voicemail.

All morning long.

By noon, my concern kicks up into a near panic. She's usually reliable. Something must be wrong. Shuffling through an old file of Uncle Steve's, I search for the application Anna must have filled out when she began working here. *Did she ever write down her home address?*

"What's up?" Gray pops his head in the door. "Everything okay?"

Why wasn't Uncle Steve more organized?

"Anna messaged me late last night and had to leave town. Something doesn't feel right; I'm worried about her. Do you know anything?"

He sighs, bracing his arms along the top of the doorframe. "Her dad's sick."

"What? How do you know that?"

"She told me."

Again, I'm reminded that Gray is so much more suited for this role than I am. People talk to him, share with him, confide in him. I don't even know where the hell Anna lives. Or where she's from.

"Damn. How bad?"

"Colon cancer. If she messaged you saying she had a family emergency, then it's most likely her dad."

"Her phone's off."

"She's probably dealing with more important things. Besides, she's from Tennessee. If she decided to drive, her phone could be dead by now."

"That makes sense." I admit, some of the panic loosening in my chest.

"Look, I'm sure she's fine. Give her a few days to get in touch with you. It's not like she flaked out. She told you she has a family emergency and has to leave town. She's got midterms coming up for her grad program, so I'm sure she'll be back. Instead of tearing your office apart looking for her home address, you should worry about how you're going to fill her shifts."

Shit. I pinch the bridge of my nose. A headache throbs behind my eyes. "For now, I'm going to have to pick them up."

"Uh, Luke, don't you think you're too busy for that?"

"Probably. But, if Anna went home for her dad, I don't

want to fill her position. It should be here for when she comes back."

"True."

"And, I don't want to go through the hiring process again. Or have to train someone new. We're just starting to gain momentum."

"Nervous you won't find another Stanton?"

I flip Gray the bird, mainly because he's right. I know I won't find another Emma. And, if I'm being honest, filling in for Anna will allow me to see more of the girl I can't stop thinking about. I'll be spending most of my evenings with Emma.

Gray snorts. "Just don't ask me to start covering for you. I'm stretched too thin."

"Seriously, fuck off."

8

EMMA

S aving the file for Senator LeBeau's speaking points, I breathe out in relief that nothing traumatic occurred in the last forty-five minutes.

Like my computer crashing.

Or Jenn announcing, "just kidding, no one cares what you think."

Or spilling coffee on my keyboard.

Or anything that would hinder the fact that I am actually submitting a briefing, in my own words, on maternal health-care reform to Jenn. And maybe, just maybe, she'll even read them.

I know, I'm dying too.

I check my email on my phone to make sure I have a copy of the file there, in the event that something traumatic happens to my office computer tonight – the office is vandal-ized, the system hacked, my computer stolen, etc. This way, the American people can rest easy knowing my briefing is safe.

Glancing at my phone for the time, it buzzes with an incoming call from Dad.

"Hey papa dukes." I ease back into my chair.

"Emmy girl." I can hear his smile through the line. "How are you? How's Jack treating you?"

I roll my eyes. Only Dad would casually call Senator LeBeau "Jack". I guess witnessing all the stupid things someone does during their college years entitles you to first name references, regardless of who you become. I'll remember this in case Lila, Mia, or Maura become famous. "Good, good. The important question is, how are you? And why are you calling me before 7:00 PM on a weekday? Aren't you juggling meetings and business trips and a crazy schedule like always?"

He chuckles, but it's forced.

"Not that I don't love a call before five!" I hurry to reassure him.

"I know. I just..." he trails off, and a huff of breath crackles through the receiver. "I need to talk to you, Em. You're the oldest and..." another heavy sigh, "I need your help."

My heart literally stops beating for like an eighth of a second, but it still feels like how I imagine a heart attack would start. "Dad, you're scaring me. Is everything okay? Is it Mom? Are you sick? Did Penny die?" My thoughts ricochet from my dad to my mom to my old faithful friend, the Stanton family golden retriever, Penny.

"No, no, nothing like that. Mom is great, and Penny is fine."

"Okay."

"Emmy, I made a bad investment. A series of bad investments," he states, his voice shaking at the end, as if he doesn't want me to know how much it's killing him to admit this out loud. My dad, Gerald Stanton, businessman extraordinaire, entrepreneur, fixer of all problems, needs help.

"It's okay, Dad," I say quickly, relieved the problem is financial and no one I love is dying. I mean, finances are fixable, right? "We can figure it out. How bad were these investments?" No one ever died from downgrading their car or cancelling a few holidays.

"We're losing the house."

I choke on my saliva. "The house?"

"Yes," he whispers.

"Does Mom know?"

"Of course." He sounds offended. Him and Mom are the ultimate team, always have been. I should have known better than to ask that. There isn't anything that my parents keep from each other, which is probably why they are the poster couple for what marriage should be like after twenty plus years. My friends always refer to them as their aspirational marrieds. #RelationshipGoals and all that. "She's going back to work." At this point, he's talking so low, I'm pressing the phone into my eardrum and still straining to hear his words.

"Work? Where? I mean, I always knew she planned on returning to the work force after she had me, but four kids kept her pretty busy."

"At a law firm. She's starting as a paralegal."

"Dad, it's okay. I mean a house is a house, you and Mom make it a home. You can do that somewhere else, right?"

"Of course."

"See?"

"There's more."

"More?"

"The real reason Mom is going back to work is to start saving for Celia's tuition."

"What about her college fund?" Alarm runs through my veins. Celia is desperate to gain acceptance to the Rhode Island School of Design and has been attending camps the last two summers to strengthen her work with ceramics and glass.

"It's gone."

"Dad," I force to gentle my tone, "what can I do to help?"

"I'm sorry, Emmy; I really am. But the next few months are going to be difficult financially. I know we promised a fun trip for after graduation and spring break, and then there's your usual allowance but... I just can't swing it anymore. Mom and I need to focus on giving Celia the same opportunities that we provided for the rest of you kids. I need you to cut up your credit cards and be more mindful of your spending. Okay?"

"Of course," I say in a rush. "I have a job now, serving, and it's going really well and I'm getting better tips and Dad, it's really fine. Don't worry about me." That was a massive stretch of the truth, but I'll figure it out. I mean, how hard could getting better tips be? I'll smile more. Or, if all else fails, cut my shirt into a lower V. I almost laugh at the thought.

"Really?" He half-laughs. "You're serving?"

I roll my eyes, absently running my fingers through my bangs. "Yeah, yeah, don't sound so surprised. I haven't dropped a tray or a bottle of wine or anything on anyone's head yet."

His laugh has more heart in it this time. "That's good, Emmy girl. Real good. I'm proud of you." And there are the golden words every little girl yearns to hear from her father. *I'm proud of you.* And I can tell from the sincerity in his voice that he is. "So, you're okay?"

"I'm great, Dad. Really. Don't worry about me. In fact, I don't need any allowance."

"That's great, Emmy. Okay then. I'm going to call Daph next. I just need all of you kids to be more mindful for the next few months. And don't worry, by the new year, we'll be back on track."

"Daddy, about the house…"

"No, I don't want you to worry about this, Emmy. I will take care of everything, especially now that I know you understand, and I can count on your support."

"Dad, of course you can count on me. I'm sorry if you ever felt like you couldn't. We'll be fine." My heart squeezes itself into my throat at the thought of my poor dad trying to juggle everything for all of us to live in our own oblivious bubbles where we have access to unlimited cash, never questioning where it's coming from. I really wish I could reach through the phone and give him a hug. And then one for Mom too. It can't be easy reentering the workforce nearly twenty-two years after you left it.

"Thank you, Emmy. That means a lot."

"I love you, Daddy."

"I love you too, Emmy girl. We'll talk soon okay?"

"Sure. 'Bye." I end the call and toss the phone next to my computer. Drawing in a deep breath, I reopen the briefing document and begin to edit and add. Right now, the only thing in my control is landing a job for after graduation.

I need to make myself indispensable.

"Just a few extra shifts," I beg Gray.

"But your margaritas aren't that good."

"They're not that bad." After replaying my conversation with Dad in my head, I calculated how much money I need to earn at Barracuda to be financially in control of my life. Not counting my tuition, let's not get crazy. I exaggerated how well the tips at Barracuda are and now, now I'm panicking. I need to make a rent payment on the first of the month and I have no clue how I'm going to do that.

"Hey," Gray leans over the bar, his eyebrows pulled together in a rare display of... concern? "I'm kidding. They're actually pretty good."

I try to smile but it falters.

His eyebrows pull tighter and he reaches forward, circling my wrist with his hand. "What's going on?"

"Nothing. I just, I need extra shifts so if you could, you know, go be a man whore at a club a few extra nights a week and give me some of your bartending shifts, I would owe you..."

"You know I get just as many numbers working here as I would at a club, right? I mean, sure the clientele is a bit different but trust me, I'm still scoring."

"Gross."

"You asked."

"I didn't need confirmation. Or that visual."

He squeezes my wrist before letting go. "Take a big gulp of this margarita and then tell me what's really going on."

I acquiesce, dropping onto a barstool and kicking my shoulder bag beneath the bar. Placing my face in my hands, I rake my fingers through my bangs. "I need the shifts because I need the money." I sip the habanero margarita and nearly choke. "It's spicy."

"Why?"

"Why? Isn't it habanero?"

"Not the margarita. Why do you need the money? You have a solid internship – I know it's not paid," he holds his hand up as I open my mouth to fill in that relevant detail, "but people don't take unpaid internships if they can't afford to."

True story. I nod.

"You dress well. I mean, hard-up interns don't tote around

Balenciaga bags and wear Jimmy Choo's, however conservative you think the heel is."

"I don't tote." I say, scowling. "And how do you even know the brands of my purse and shoes?"

"What's going on? Are you in some kind of trouble?"

"No, not trouble. I just," *God, he's going to make me say it,* "I need to earn more money. Some things came up with my family and I," *just say it Emma!* "I need to help my parents out, okay?"

Gray stops shaking the second margarita he's mixing up and places the shaker on the bar. "Oh."

"Yeah."

"So you're just trying to help out your family?"

I nod.

"Wow."

"Wow?" *Why am I always repeating things other people say?*

"I just didn't expect you to say that. That's very… noble of you."

I snort.

"I'm serious. Most twenty-one-year-olds wouldn't have that type of emotional maturity. Or care, to be honest." He picks the shaker back up and pours the margarita into a glass, adding a colorful umbrella.

"Speaking from experience?"

"Actually, I am. You can take my Wednesday nights and join me behind the bar on Saturdays from 9:00 PM until we close. I'll have to clear it with Luke, but I'm sure it won't be a problem. The truth is, we'd have to find someone soon anyway. Saturday nights are picking up, and I could use the help. We'll split tips. Plus, it'll be more fun."

"Really? That would be great," I gush, standing up on the barstool rung and leaning over to hug Gray.

"Ah Em, no need to be such a softie," he says, crushing me to his chest. "What you're doing, it's cool of you."

"Thanks Gray." I stand up, balancing, more like teetering, on the rung of the barstool.

"What's going on?" Luke's deep voice startles me, and I lose my footing.

Except before I can faceplant, his arm snakes around my waist and pulls me flush against his chest. Hard muscles cut in between my shoulder blades as I breathe in his cologne and practically melt into him. His hand splays across my stomach and with any other man, say, Josh McCannon, I'd feel incredibly self-conscious. But with Luke, it feels right.

Jesus, what is wrong with you?

I start to sit back down but Luke holds me in place.

His stubble prickles my ear as he drops his chin. "You okay, Emma?"

I nod, my breath coming out in little puffs of oxygen. "I'm fine. Thanks for the save."

He slides onto the barstool next to mine, keeping a hand on my lower back. The heat from his palm seeps through my shirt and I nearly shiver from the awareness.

Oh God, what is wrong with me? I've never reacted this way to a simple touch before. But with Luke, every glance, every shoulder brush, every everything feels like so much more.

"I just asked Em if she could pick up my Wednesday nights and join me for a bit on Saturday nights." Gray explains, reminding me that he's still here.

I look up, opening my mouth to explain that I need the shifts but Gray shakes his head.

"Oh yeah?" Luke picks up Gray's discarded margarita and takes a sip. His face contorts in disgust. And he looks adorable. Le sigh. "Corona please."

Gray pulls out a beer and pops the top, wedging in a lime slice. "I'm trying something new."

"It's spicy."

"Habanero." Gray swivels his hips suggestively and grins at me.

"Gross." I take another sip of my drink. "You, not the margarita."

Luke snorts and takes a pull of his beer. "So, Wednesday and Saturday nights? You sure it's not too much for your schedule?"

"Nope. It'll be great." *Please let me have the extra nights.*

Luke shrugs. "It's your twenties."

"That's what I told her; but at least I'll have extra time now to enjoy mine." Gray holds up his margarita, "Cheers."

"Cheers."

I'm exhausted.

So fucking tired that my eyes ache, even when they're closed. Wiping down another table near the back of Barracuda, I'm relieved it's almost closing time. I straighten a chair and scan the area to make sure all the tables are clean when my cell rings from the office. Glancing at Emma, she waves me away, chatting with a couple of girls at the bar.

"Hello?"

"Luke?"

"Yeah. Who's this?"

"Scoop Rayes."

"Scoop Rayes? For real?" Surprise colors my voice and I can't decide if Scoop Rayes, the coach who watched me spar with Manny last week, is really calling me or if Toby put one of the guys up to pranking the shit out of me.

He chuckles, which is confusing because Scoop Rayes doesn't strike me as a warm person. He's got a poker face all the time and mean mugs anyone who looks at him for a beat too long. "It's me, man."

"Hey. What can I do for you?"

"The better question is, what can I do for you? I hear you're looking to go pro."

"Jesus, hell yeah. I want to go pro." *But can I?* I can't drop everything at Barracuda to train. *How can I fit in that type of commitment to training and unwavering dedication to my diet and keep things running here?*

"I watched you spar at The Cellar last week. I was impressed. I think you got what it takes, kid."

"Thank you. I, I'd love to go pro but I'm not sure I can right now. Jesus, Scoop, I want nothing more. Going pro has been my dream since I was a kid, and if you called me a few months back, I'd be shitting myself to train with you. Fuck, I am shitting myself."

"What changed?"

I tug on the back of my neck as I tell him the truth that none of the other guys I used to roll with know. I mean, I'm sure they heard through the grapevine, but I haven't been open about it. "My uncle passed. He was more like a father to me and –"

"Shit, son. I'm sorry to hear that."

"Yeah, well, he left me his restaurant."

"And?"

"And now I'm running it and I can't just turn my back on it because it's his legacy and means a lot to my mom and –"

"You're stuck."

"Like fucking crazy glue."

"I respect that. I do. But you gotta think about your dream and your future too. Opportunities like this, they're not going to come around often. There's a fight against Joe Carney happening in December, right before the holidays. I know this is short notice for you, but it's a super fight, big time, pay per view, all the bells and whistles. Opportunity of a lifetime, won't come by again."

"Yeah, he's supposed to be fighting Nicky Nova," I interrupt, referencing the big fight that's been in the works for the past eighteen months. A title shot, contender Nicky Nova is going after Joe "Lightning" Carney's belt. It's the fight of a lifetime, the real deal.

"Got caught doping," Scoop throws out. "He fucked himself over. There's no room for that shit at this level. Anyway, talking to Frankie and Toby and some other guys, your name kept getting thrown into the ring. This fight's been in the works for a long time, and way too much money has been thrown down to cancel it. We're looking for contenders to replace Nova, and I want to back you. I've watched you fight, man, not just last week at The Cellar. I've had my eye on you for a while. Even though you'd be a fringe contender, you've got the raw potential to be a formidable challenger. You're good, really good. But I can make you the best. If you want this, really fucking want it, come train under me."

A fight against Joe Carney? Against Lightning himself? Shit. Nothing like showing someone their dream is within reach and then snatching it away at the last second. It's like taking food out from under a dog's nose. Cruel.

I blow out another breath, tugging harder on my neck, my heart and head split over what I should do. What I want to do and what is the right thing to do. "I appreciate that, Scoop. I really do. Your even calling me means a lot. Can I have some time to think about it? See what I can work out on my end? I'd love a shot to fight Lightning but I need to make sure I can make the commitment first."

"Yeah man. Of course. Don't wait too long, though. If it's not for you, I gotta look for another fighter. And we gotta move fast. This opening isn't going to last, and Lightning's management team is desperate to fill it. Can't be losing his contract outright. Too much dough on the line."

"Yeah. Okay. Thanks."

"One more thing. Win or lose, it's $300,000 in your pocket. In case you got some financial concerns to consider."

He clicks off before I can react, and I sag in my desk chair, a confusing hurricane of emotions sweeping through me.

Adrenaline spikes in my veins. *I can do this; I know I can.*

Scoop Rayes wants to train me.

Me!

To fight the current heavyweight champion.

In the professional boxing circuit.

It's the opportunity of a lifetime, the chance to pursue something I've dreamt about, worked at, sweated for since I was a kid.

And I could pay back Uncle P the loan money outright. Even if I don't win.

That thought cracks me up. *They're going to pay me that much money just for showing up? How could I not take this opportunity?*

My high dies a thousand deaths as reality sifts into my thoughts.

What happens to Barracuda in the meantime?

Who keeps things running?

Can I risk Uncle Steve's legacy for my own dream?

I've never wanted anything so desperately in my life as I want to pursue this opportunity.

Scrubbing my fingers over my eyes, the weight of such an important decision causes the exhaustion to settle deeper, and I swear to God I could fall asleep right here, sitting in this uncomfortable chair, and not move until morning.

A knock near the door forces me to open my eyes and sit up straight.

"Hey." Emma dawdles in the doorframe. Exhaustion lines her face but a smile curves her lips. *Is she always happy and smiling?*

"What's up?"

"I closed out my last table, and the girls from the bar just left."

"Yeah, okay."

"Do you want me to close out the registers, or do you want to do it?"

"I'll do it. You can head out if you want."

"Okay. See you tomorrow."

Dropping my head back, I try to mentally psych myself to wake up so I can close out the registers and fill out the deposit slips for the bank. Pushing up from the desk, I hear Emma shuffling around in the restaurant, so I force myself to walk out of the office so I can say goodnight and stop acting like a braindead dick.

She's already near the door, her bag slung over her shoulder, when I see her reach into her back pocket and fish out a metro card.

"You're taking the metro?"

"Hm? Yeah."

"But it's almost midnight." I track her body, my eyes lingering on her curves more than they should. *Jesus, she can't walk around DC at night, alone and vulnerable.*

"I know. I need to hurry so I don't miss the connection at Metro Center."

"Give me fifteen; I'll take you home."

She waves a hand at me, rolling her eyes. "You don't have to do that. I'll make it. 'Night Luke."

Alarm spikes through me as her fingers graze the doorknob. "Emma, please. Let me drive you. It's not safe this time of night, and I'd hate it if you missed the connection and were sitting in the station by yourself, then standing outside waiting for an Uber or trying to catch a cab." I gulp air, imagining the easy target sweet Emma would make, standing on a dark corner alone. "I'd do the same for any of my employees. Except maybe Gray."

She rolls her eyes again but this time, her grin is playful. "Alright, alright, you can have the honor of driving me home."

"It'd be my pleasure." I joke but my voice is too deep, my tone too gruff. Clearing my throat, I add, "Just give me a few."

She drops her bag on one of the tables and walks toward me, stepping behind the bar. "It'll be faster if we do it together." She explains, pulling up the POS software on the monitor.

I stand behind her, distracted by her enthusiasm, her innocence, her ass. *What is it about Emma Stanton?*

"Luke?"

"Hm."

"Want to do the other register?"

"Uh, yeah. On it." I mumble, stepping beside her and pulling up the software.

Even as I run the numbers, I know I'll need to double check everything tomorrow morning. Because Emma's presence, alone in an empty Barracuda, more than distracts me. She overwhelms me, pulling me closer, weakening my resistance, showing me a sliver of "what could be" instead of "what is."

And damn it, I want it.

I want it all.

"JUST TELL ME WHERE TO TURN."

"Oh, yeah, make a right two streets after the next light." She points out the window and turns to look at me. "Everything okay?"

"Yeah. Why?"

"You seem distracted. Quieter than normal. I just thought maybe –"

"What if someone pretty much put your dream on a silver platter in front of you and all you had to do was reach out and take it, but it would mean pissing some people off and hurting others?"

"I'd take it."

"But you would hurt people you care about."

"If they're people I truly care about, don't they care about me?"

"Of course."

"Then they should want me to be happy and to achieve my dream."

Damn. That's a good point.

"And, even if I was hurting them in some way, I'd explain why I'm making the decision I am, make them understand why it's so important to me. Then, they should encourage me to go for it if they care about me as much as I care about them. Otherwise, these aren't people whose opinions I'd consider anyway." She adds.

Also true. I know deep down Mom would support me. She knows this is what I've always wanted. The only problem is that my mom isn't herself at the moment. And Uncle Steve is gone so I can't even ask him, although he too would encourage me to go for it, even at the loss of his restaurant. He would point out that his dream isn't my dream and it isn't supposed to be.

God, I know all of this. *So why is it still so hard to make the decision?*

"Don't make any decisions tonight," Emma grasps my forearm and I drop my hand from the steering wheel, letting it rest on the center console between us. "You're tired. And obviously stressed about the whole thing. Sleep on it. Reevaluate in the morning. But if it was me and my dream was within reach, I wouldn't hesitate."

"What is your dream?" I glance at her from the corner of my eye, curious for any information she wants to share.

"You first."

"I got a title shot. The match is set in December, against the current champion. It's the chance of a lifetime, especially for someone like me who isn't even in the professional circuit but wants to be."

She nods for several seconds before grinning sheepishly. "I have no clue what you're talking about. What does that mean? A title shot?"

I laugh, pulling my forearm back so I can lace my fingers with hers. *Jesus, I'm holding her hand.* Like a twelve-year-old. And yet, my blood warms the same way it did when I was crushing on a girl in middle school. "I'm a boxer."

"A boxer?"

"You're surprised."

She snorts, "Uh, yeah. A little."

"Do you think I should take the fight?"

"Depends. How good are you?"

I chuckle, squeezing her fingers. "Damn. What, you don't think I can fight?"

She shrugs but her eyes are bright, lit up like Christmas lights.

"I'm pretty good or they wouldn't have offered me the

spot. And it's a legit gig. No more bareknuckle boxing in parking lots for bets."

"You're really a boxer? Like for real?"

"For real."

"And you let people hit you without any gloves on?"

"Hopefully not anymore."

"This is your dream? To have a big fight and win a title or whatever?"

"Yeah." I chuckle. "This is pretty much the dream of everyone who wants to be a professional boxer."

"Then take it."

I blow out a breath, chewing the corner of my mouth. "What's your dream?"

She starts to slide her fingers from mine but I tighten my grip, looking over at her.

"It's silly." She wrinkles her nose.

"I told you I let people hit me."

"True. Okay, I want to work on issues I care about, to make a difference in the lives of others, to do something that helps people." She faces the window again before turning back to me. "I'm sure that sounds naive and ignorant, but I want to do something I believe in, something that matters for other people. Something that matters to me."

"That's not silly. And you're not naive." I swipe my thumb over the back of her hand, almost groaning at how soft her skin is. Jesus, I need to get a grip. Dropping her fingers, I regrip the steering wheel and turn right. "What you want to do, who you are," I risk a quick glance in her direction, "I think it's beautiful. You're special, Emma. Different from any other girl I know."

"Thank you," she says, a blush working its way across her cheeks. "Third building on the left."

Slowing my SUV to make a quick U-turn, I park in front of her building. "Is that why you picked DC? The Hill?"

"Yes. I'm desperate to land a job for after graduation."

"Then you will."

"How can you be so sure?"

"Stay starving for what you want. Work for it. It's not a guarantee but with most things, I've found that if you're hungry enough, you'll eventually eat."

"Is that how you feel about boxing? Like you're starving?"

I nod, shifting in my seat so I'm facing her. "Like I can't breathe in oxygen fast enough. That's how badly I want it."

One corner of her mouth ticks up as she fiddles with her bangs, sweeping them across her forehead and out of her eyes. "I've always wondered what it would feel like to be that passionate about something."

"Sounds like you're very passionate about your work."

"I am. But not like I can't breathe. If you feel that much intensity for boxing, you're lucky to have discovered you're passion. You can't say no to this opportunity."

"I know."

"Then why are you second guessing it?"

"Barracuda."

She furrows her brow, silently asking for more information.

I sigh, tapping my head back against the window. "My uncle passed over the summer. Barracuda was his baby and he left her to me and now…"

"You want it to be everything he wanted it to be."

"Exactly. And it's important to my mom."

Emma nods, staring at me for so long, I shift my weight again. Her eyes are soft, thoughtful. The air between us constricts as the silence grows heavier. Unable to withstand the tension a moment longer, I lean forward, dropping an elbow to the center console.

"Emma."

"You're a good man, Luke."

A chuckle that lacks warmth, lacks humor, rips from my throat as I shake my head. "No I'm not, babe. I'm not even close."

Confusion sparks in Emma's eyes as she leans closer, a moth to a flame. Her fingers graze the skin of my arm but her eyes are hard. "Don't say that. There aren't many men who would even consider what you are. Not taking your shot at a dream because of your uncle's legacy, because of how much you love your mom. Anyone who puts their family first like that is a good person, Luke."

Something squeezes in my chest at her words, a vise gripping down until my breathing shallows. *What the hell does she* see *in me? And why can't I see it?*

"Why Lone Wolf?" she asks, jutting her chin toward the tattoos across my knuckles.

"Been on my own a long time."

The corner of Emma's mouth tips up as she takes my hand and dips her head. My breath literally catches in my throat and I forget to breathe. Because she kisses my knuckles.

She kisses my calloused, swollen, split knuckles covered in ink like they're goddamn beautiful.

It's a simple act, a sweet gesture. But her innocence coupled with all the confusing emotions I feel for her has my blood raging like a hurricane, my mind twisting like a tornado.

Emma looks up at me under her bangs, her eyes big and beautiful and so goddamn trusting that I snap.

Reaching across the stupid center console, I wrap my

hands around her upper arms and tug her forward until my mouth clashes with hers.

Our kiss isn't sweet or soft or innocent.

It's heady and wild and filled with too much promise to be anything but a flame that will burn out.

Still, when a moan drops from her lips, I don't rip myself away like I know I should. I deepen the kiss, press my tongue into her open mouth and let it melt with hers.

I kiss Emma Stanton with reckless abandon because she *sees* me.

And that makes me a special kind of selfish.

Because I don't deserve her. Or her sweetness. Her innocence. Her goddamn softness.

But fuck me if I'm not going to take it all.

OCTOBER

10

EMMA

I t's late when my phone rings.

Reaching over to the nightstand blindly, I fumble my Kindle and glasses before my fingers wrap around the cord of the charger. Squinting at the phone screen, Lila's face and name clears from the blur of my tragic vision.

"Emma?"

"Li? Hey, what's up? You okay?" I clear the sleep from my throat, sitting up in bed and turning on the bedside lamp.

"Oh Emma, I'm so sorry! I keep forgetting about the time difference."

"Lila, what's wrong?" I ask the second I see her blood-shot, red-rimmed eyes.

"It's Cade. He got injured in the game last weekend, a broken tibia."

"Oh God." I lean forward, pressing my face closer to the phone as if that could press me closer to my best friend. "I'm so sorry to hear that. How's he holding up?"

"I think okay. I don't know. I just have this awful feeling that something else is going on. I mean, it's been almost a week and he's still in the hospital. Isn't that weird? Why would they keep someone that long for a broken leg?"

"I don't know, Li. He's an athlete. Maybe the protocol is different."

"I guess."

"Are you okay? You look like you've been crying."

Tears well in her eyes. "I can't shake this feeling that something bad is about to happen. I feel like Cade's avoiding me."

"Lila, I'm sure everything is okay. You told me Cade had huge dreams for the NFL. If he broke his leg, his dream was just pulled away from him not even a week ago and he's probably processing everything. Not to mention I'm sure he's in a lot of physical pain and doped up on meds."

She sighs, a finger twirling and tugging her hair. "Yeah, that makes sense."

"Just give him some time. Things between you guys have been scorching hot. Trust me, he's not going anywhere, he's just sorting his shit out."

"Hope so." She smiles shakily. "I miss you."

"I miss you too. A lot."

"Tell me what's going on in your life. Who's that guy you're taking shots with in the Facebook photo?"

I snort, remembering a photo Gray tagged me in, uploaded to Barracuda's business page. Awkwardly enough, I'm taking a shot of Diet Coke. "My co-worker Gray. He's a pain in the ass."

"He looks like he's got a great ass."

"You wouldn't notice the second he opens his mouth."

"He's a jerk?"

"Oh, no. I adore him. He's quickly becoming one of my friends."

"Ah, friend zoned."

"Exactly."

"Well, if the guys in DC look like that, I can't imagine you're having a tough time sticking to our pact."

"I got a serving job."

Her surprise is evident as her eyebrows lift nearly to her hairline. "You're waitressing?"

"I am."

"Why? I mean, wouldn't you rather be at the party than working it?"

"I'm pushing past my comfort zone, having a different kind of adventure."

"Okay." She draws the words out, not buying my response.

"And, my boss is hot as fuck and I may or may not have made out with him in his car just two nights ago when he drove me home."

"Finally, I understand!" Lila squeals, giggling like a psycho. "God, Em, you had me worried for a second."

"Hold up," I lift a palm. "That's not why I took the job. But, I'm so glad I did because Luke is so hot. And, wait for it, he's a boxer. Like a real one."

"Damn." Lila says, her eyes taking on a faraway look. "What happened after the kiss?"

"I got out of his car. I just hope things aren't awkward between us now at work."

"Since he's the boss?"

"That, and we do spend a lot of time working together. He recently took over his late uncle's restaurant so he's there a lot."

"I'm sure it will be fine. You have nothing to feel awkward about; if anything, he does. He's the boss."

"Truth. So, despite the horrible injury, how are things with you and Cade?"

Lila's face transforms at the mention of Cade. Her cheeks blush pink and her eyes soften. "I really like him." Her fingers cover her mouth and I know, really know, that she's in love with him.

"You're emanating sunshine and rainbows."

"I don't even care."

"Damn, girl. Gush away."

She does; Lila tells me all about Cade's abs, the grey thundercloud color of his eyes, and how he makes her feel like home.

I tell her all about Luke's blazing green eyes, sexy tattoos, and breathtaking smile.

We talk for over an hour and it isn't until after I hang up that I realize neither one of us mentioned our internships. At all.

But I can't lose sight of why I'm really here. I need to find a job for after graduation.

A paying job.

And as much as I want Luke to distract me seven ways from Sunday, I can't let him distract me from my goal.

"YOU'RE BEING LAME." Cassie tells me, her mouth wide open as she applies a second coat of mascara and tries not to poke herself in the eye.

"I know," I flip the pages of the October issue of *Cosmopolitan*. There once was a time when I could spot the new trends and enjoy a shopping excursion the next day, making sure my wardrobe was on point for the season.

Those days are long gone.

"Just come with me. I promise you'll have fun." She

stares at me through the mirror and I look up, meeting her gaze.

"Trust me, I'd love to come. I really would. I just…" *How do I explain that I'm broke?*

"Look," Cassie cuts me off when my pause hangs between us, "I don't know you that well. And I see how ridiculously hard you're working, which I admire. But I want to go out tonight and I don't know anyone else and I don't want to go alone so really, you'd be doing me a favor if you just came with me. I can spot us both and," she holds her hand up, silencing the protests I am about to unleash, "the money isn't a big deal for me. So please, come with me."

Rolling my eyes, I remember all the times I said the same thing to my friends. On nights when Maura wanted to stay in because she didn't have the funds for a night out that would undoubtedly end with bottle service at a club, I would drag her along, telling her the money didn't matter, her company did. And now Cassie is doing that for me.

"Cass, I just feel –"

"I know," she cuts me off again, turning to look at me, "guilty and awkward. But I don't care. I feel bored and want to have a night out with my roommate. So get up and get dressed, because you're coming even if I have to drag you by your hair."

"Did anyone ever tell you you're kind of scary when you want your way?"

"All the time." She turns back to the mirror. "We're leaving in thirty, so go get ready."

I drop the magazine on her bed, debating what to do.

But I'm desperate to go out.

I need a girl's night, a night to have some fun with a friend. *Am I being selfish? Or, is this karma repaying me for all the times I've spotted my friends? Oh my God, stop justi-*

fying it. The truth is that I probably shouldn't go out, but I'm going to anyway. And I'm going to owe Cassie.

"Thank you," I call out, beelining to my bedroom.

"If you want to repay me, just drink a lot of shots and dance your ass off tonight, yeah?"

"Done!"

Flipping through the hangars in my closet like a crazy person, I search for the perfect outfit. This could very well be one of my one nights out in DC this semester.

A HIP-HOP SONG I don't recognize but immediately want to learn bumps through the speaker as Cassie and I walk through the door of the club. Sweet sweat and stale beer clings to my clothes and weaves through my hair as I push through the medley of bodies to the bar, dragging Cassie behind me.

My God. I've missed this.

Inhaling, I relish the scents that would normally cause my nose to wrinkle in disgust. *Ah, alcohol and poor decisions. It's been ages, my old friends.*

"Damn I wish I wore wedges instead of these." Cassie grumbles as we reach the bar. She leans forward to give her feet a reprieve from her ridiculous-but-oh-so-fabulous four-inch candy apple red stilettos.

"Your dress deserves the heels." I wave my hand in front of her tight, short, black dress that clings to all the right curves. "You're hot."

She rolls her eyes, plucking a discarded coaster off the bar and fanning herself with it. "I am hot. I feel like I'm gonna melt into a puddle on the floor if we don't get drinks soon."

"Patience is a virtue," I remind her, stretching out my arm and standing on my tippy toes to catch the bartender's eye.

Success.

I still got it!

"What can I get you girls?" He asks in a delicious Australian accent that has Cassie straightening on her heels and pushing her chest out.

It's all you, girl.

I step back slowly, allowing her to occupy more space at the bar and order our drinks. Cassie's a fantastic flirt. It never hurts to pick up a few pointers.

Within minutes, Cassie is pressing a mojito into my hand. Flipping her hair over her shoulder, she laughs as Aussie lines up three shot glasses and fills them with chilled vodka, pushing a napkin with sugared lemons in our direction. Lemon drops.

I pick up a shot glass and raise it toward Aussie and Cassie before throwing it back and biting into the lemon, desperately failing at not recalling the tangy lime I bit into just a few nights earlier.

"I'm off at two." Aussie calls out over his shoulder as he walks down the bar to another customer.

"I'll see you then." Cassie replies, turning to face me. "And that," she pauses as she touches the corner of her mouth with a bar napkin, careful not to smudge her lipstick, "is how it's done."

"Good thing you wore the heels. Come on, let's dance."

CASSIE and I are falling over each other between the alcohol making our thoughts fuzzy and the waves of giggles erupting from our lipstick-stained mouths. *Why are we laughing?* I can't remember. All I know is that once we started, neither of us could stop.

I miss nights like these.

Back at McShain, it's usually just Lila and me getting into this much fun as Maura always has rowing and Mia is way too dedicated to ballet and would never consume the number of calories in sugary drinks – not to mention the 3AM pizza we always order. But still, being out among people, dancing wildly, laughing hysterically, is just the remedy I need to lessen the stress I've been carrying around since Dad's phone call.

Cassie presses her fingertips to the corners of her eyes and dabs at the tears that gathered there.

"You're so proper!"

"You're a hot mess," she laughs back.

"You better freshen up in time for your hot date," I continue, trying to mimic Aussie's accent and failing.

"I'll be right back." She gestures toward the women's bathroom.

"I'm going to grab another round," I tell her, forgetting all about my money issues in this moment. This is why people like me shouldn't drink. I tend to make the poor decision. "Meet me back at the bar?"

"Get some shots too."

I laugh, watching her walk-slash-limp to the bathroom. Her feet must be killing her after all the dancing we did, but still, she's holding it together pretty well.

At the bar, I flag down a different bartender and order a couple of mojitos and Patron shots.

"Add it to my tab."

I look up, mesmerized by Luke's deep green eyes.

"Hey."

"Hi." He smiles now, his entire face transforming.

"You don't have to." I gesture toward the drinks as the

bartender slides them in front of me and Luke signals for more shots.

"Who're you drinking with?"

"Cassie. My roommate."

Luke nods.

"She's just in the bathroom," I continue, unable to stop myself from blabbering now that we're outside of work, in the same space, having an actual conversation. And, let's be real, I'm fairly tipsy. Funny how a bit of vodka and tequila can loosen the tongue and all that.

"Well, let's at least have a shot while you wait for her." Luke grins again, and I'm nearly blinded by the perfection of his features. He slides a shot glass in front of me.

"To the start of new dreams," I lift my shot.

"New dreams."

I take the shot. It burns a delicious trail of heat down my throat, into my stomach, fanning out through my arms and legs.

The warm touch of Luke's fingers on the corner of my mouth has me inhaling sharply and forgetting to breathe all at the same time. I freeze as he wipes away a drop of tequila that settled there.

"Do you come here often?" His eyes never leave my face. His hand flutters slowly from my mouth, grazing my shoulder, briefly touching my elbow, before returning to the bar.

I shake my head, my thoughts caught up on our kiss from the other night. *Is he going to kiss me again? Please kiss me again!*

"There you are!" Cassie stumbles into me and I lurch forward, more into Luke's personal space. His hands shoot out to steady me and he turns me until my back rests against the bar, my body framed nicely in between his thighs as he swivels back and forth on the barstool, his knees tapping out a rhythm against my lower back and abdomen.

I act cool. You know, chill. Ha! My insides are melting like hot lava, and I have to remind myself to breathe.

"I've been looking for you forever." Cassie takes another step toward the bar to look over my shoulder. "I love tequila!" She squeals, picking up the shot glass waiting for her.

"Cass." I place a hand on her arm, "This is Luke. Luke, Cassie."

Luke leans forward on the barstool, the top of his shoulder bumping against mine. "Good to meet you." His voice is low, even.

Cassie's eyes widen, and a slow smirk plays across her lips. *Oh, brother. Did she already forget about her "date" with the Aussie?*

"You too. Do you come here a lot? I've never seen you before."

Let me just add that Cassie has been here on one other occasion. When a bunch of people she interns with at the EPA decided to celebrate one of the girl's birthdays. I again fight the urge to roll my eyes at her.

Luke chuckles, leaning back on the barstool, his hand coming up to grasp the back of my neck, his fingers squeezing. "Not really. I was just asking Em here the same question."

Em? Who the hell is Em? Is he nicknaming me?

Let's be real, pretty much everyone I know calls me Em. But it sounds so different, so much... better... when Luke says it. My insides feel squishy.

"My cousin dragged me," he continues, "It's not really my scene."

Gray is here?

"What is your scene?" Cassie, obviously focused on the

more important aspects of that statement, asks in a flirty, breathless, voice, her eyes focused on me. *Ah yes, she's doing me a solid. Opening the conversation up so I can jump in.* Except I can't. I'm frozen. An icicle. Staring at the only man that renders me speechless.

Until the one that causes me to word vomit barges his way into our little circle.

"Emma Stanton, drinking *and* dancing? Who are you? And why haven't I met your beautiful friend?"

I swat Gray in the stomach. "This is my roommate Cassie. Cass, Gray."

"Pleasure's all mine, darlin'.'"

"Turning on that country charm, are ya? And, I thought you were from Connecticut."

"Quit it, Stanton, or I'll whisk your friend away and leave you with this ogre." Gray gestures toward Luke.

I laugh and as the song changes, Gray's face lights up. "Cassie," he offers Cassie his arm like he's a gentleman at a ball and not a playboy in a dark club, "may I have this dance?"

"Certainly, sir." Cassie plays along, giggling.

Within moments, the swell of bodies pulsing around us swallows them up.

And it's just me, Luke, and tequila.

11

LUKE

S he's drunk.
Obviously so.

And yet, it's disarming in a way I can't explain.

She's not lewd and dramatic, demanding the attention of every guy in the club, like the fangirls I'm used to. She's not trying to chat me up for free drinks or an invitation to my bed. She's just herself. And that quiet confidence is a hell of a lot sexier than lacey lingerie or fake tits.

The memory of kissing her plays with my mind more than all the fangirls I've banged in dirty alleyways over the past year.

"So, Luke…"

"How's your internship going? Any closer to landing that job?"

Emma brightens, a smile stretching across her full lips as she grips the bar to steady herself. "I love it. Senator LeBeau is awesome. I mean, he's such a politician." She rolls her eyes and cuts her gaze to me, "But he really cares, you know? He believes in the legislation he's working on and it's rewarding to be a part of that. I hope I can convince him to offer me a job for after graduation. I'd love to stay on in his office."

"What issues is he championing?" I know absolutely nothing about Senator LeBeau, but knowing Uncle P, I can only guess he's championing his own self-interests to gain status, wealth, and a misplaced sense of superiority.

"Refugee resettlement, parental leave, immigration reform." She ticks off her fingers, raising her voice so I can hear her over the music.

"That's an impressive list."

"And it's not even all of it." Emma flips her hair over her shoulder, color blooming in her cheeks as her passion comes to life. "He's committed to developing legislation for so many important issues that could help improve the lives for thousands of people. I mean, can you even believe that we live in a developed country and women here are only granted twelve measly weeks of unpaid leave after they give birth?" She takes another step forward, settling nicely in between my thighs. "Unpaid! How are families supposed to support another human being in the earliest days of the baby's life without a salary? And how is three months enough time for parents to bond with their child and establish their own routine before having to sort out childcare? And don't even get me started on the cost of daycare..." Her eyes widen and a blush works up her throat. "God, sorry, I don't mean to ramble. It just drives me crazy. It's like the government doesn't want families to have children with the lack of support provided."

I reach out and tuck a strand of hair behind her ear, loving that she leans into my touch. "Don't be sorry. It's important to care about things that are bigger than yourself. I haven't seen anyone so impassioned by a real issue in a long time." I can't help my mind from wandering back to my own mother, the issues she championed once upon a time, the beautiful idealism she wore like a cloak. But that was before dad died and she saw Uncle P for who he is. "Is everyone in your family like you? Out to save the world? Or do you just drive your siblings crazy with all your good-doer deeds?"

"Definitely not. My sister Daphne is a straight-up party girl, Jon's a player, and Celia's an artist. Even my best friends think I'm nuts half the time."

"What are they like? Your friends."

Her eyes take on a glassy look, as if she's reliving a memory. "I miss them."

"Why don't they come visit? I mean, Gray told me you're at college in Philadelphia, right?"

"Yeah," she nods, "but only Maura is there this semester." She looks at me over her shoulder before turning so that she's facing me. "There are four of us, we all dormed together freshman year. This is the first semester we've ever been apart. Lila, she's my best friend, is kind of like the offspring of a hippie and a frat boy. She's fun and wild and daring. But super smart, annoyingly so. She's in LA for the semester doing a medical internship. She's already fallen in love with a football player." Emma rolls her eyes at this, laughing. "Mia is in Rome. Now that's a place I'd like to visit. She's on a study abroad and I'm pretty sure she's falling for an Italian. But really, who could blame her? And Maura…"

"The one still in Philadelphia?"

"Right," Emma nods. "She's an athlete, women's rowing. It's stupid how early she has to get up for practice but she's super committed so a semester away wasn't in the cards for her."

"It sounds like you're really close."

"We are; they're the best. But I definitely lucked out with Cassie as my roomie for this semester."

"Yeah, she seems cool."

"She is. What about you? Do you have roommates?"

"Nah," I shake my head. "I'm on my own."

"The Lone Wolf?"

"Exactly."

Emma chews her bottom lip, drawing my attention to the movement. Jesus, her mouth is perfect. Our kiss still sears the edges of my memory, making me want to capture her mouth right here. Claim her in front of this entire club of people. "That must be nice, never having to wait for the bathroom."

Snorting, I admit, "I never thought about that."

"You would if you had three siblings at home and three roommates at school."

"Fair enough. You having fun tonight?"

"I had a great time." Emma sways, gripping my arm for balance. "But I'm pretty beat. Think I'm going to call it." She leans forward, her chest colliding with mine as she places her hands on my shoulders and kisses the corner of my mouth. Jesus. "Thanks for the drink, Luke."

"Emma, wait. How are you and Cassie getting home?" *Because there's no way in hell I'm letting you walk away from me in the middle of a club, drunk and vulnerable, with a bunch of guys circling you like sharks.*

"Oh, I'm just going to grab a cab. Or an Uber. Cassie has... plans."

"I'll take you."

"You don't have to cut your night short."

"I want to take you." I signal to the bartender to close out my tab.

"Careful Luke, you're good man deeds are starting to become a habit."

Chuckling, I sign my bill and slip my credit card into my wallet. "Dance with me, babe."

"What? You dance?"

"Every now and then," I lace my fingers with hers and guide us toward the dance floor. As the song changes to a low, languid beat, I pull Emma closer and hold her against my chest, crossing all kinds of lines again. No fucks given.

She comes willingly, molding herself around me as if she was meant to fit into my arms. My hands are splayed wide on either side of her waist and I love the dip my fingers effortlessly curl into. Her head fits perfectly underneath my chin and I breathe her in. Coconut and sweetness. An innocence that's too good, too pure, for a man like me to savor.

Emma turns her head, placing her cheek against my shoulder. Her steps slow and I know she's exhausted.

Pulling my phone from my back pocket, I text Gray.

Me: Emma is done. Going to give her a ride. Are you still with her roommate?

Gray: Yeah. She's up for staying out. Has a hot date with a bartender after close. I'll keep an eye on her 'til then.

Me: Cool. Talk later.

The song fades into another track, the tempo of the music increasing as couples drunkenly stagger back from each other.

"Come on," I whisper, keeping an arm wrapped around Emma and guiding her off the dance floor. "Let's get you home."

She glances up, her eyelids hooded. "My place or yours?"

"Emma."

"Luke."

I touch my forehead to hers. "If you and me do…things, we can't keep pretending there's nothing between us."

"I hate pretending anything."

Sweeping my thumb over her cheekbone, I kiss her lips softly. The way I should have the first time. "Mine."

She grins, dropping her head back to my shoulder.

"But tonight, all we do is sleep." I add.

Her gaze cuts up again.

"You're pretty tipsy, babe."

Emma snorts, nodding her consent, and I guide her out of the bar. Outside, a rush of cold air hits us and I pull her tighter into my side. There's no way she isn't cold in the short, backless navy dress she's wearing. Modest from the front, I moaned the first time she turned around. Emma is unassuming when you first meet her. But after that first smile, she transforms into a beauty so classic and sweet, it's impossible not to stare.

Helping her into my SUV, I click in her seatbelt. She grins as my fingers trail over her hip, tugging on the belt to make sure she's secure. We're not too far from my apartment and a strange sensation ripples through my chest the closer we get to my place.

I've never taken a woman I know home before. Sure, I've had the fangirls and the random one-night stands. But no one like Emma. No one that matters.

What will she think of my place?

Nerves that I've never anticipated unleash in my veins, calling forward a thousand questions I don't have the answers to. Shit. Gripping the steering wheel, I cut Emma a look and laugh.

Because while I'm freaking out in the driver's seat, Emma is passed out on the passenger side.

By the time I park my SUV, a gentle snore flutters from her nose. And even that is cute.

"Come on babe, we're here."

She blinks at me slowly, as if she can't tell if I'm real or not. A hand reaches out and her fingertips trail down the side of my face, from my temple to my chin, before dropping back in her lap.

"Emma?"

Silence.

"Let's get you to bed, babe." I reach into the car and pick her up, cradling her against my chest.

Her eyes are closed when she rests her head against my shoulder. She breathes in deep, a soft sigh escaping her lips. Carrying her into my building, I take the elevator up to my floor. Once inside my apartment, I settle her on my bed, brushing her bangs out of her eyes.

Sleeping Emma is peaceful, sweet, and so damn beautiful. I run my thumb over her cheekbone and press a kiss to her cheek before unclasping her shoes and tugging my comforter over her shoulders.

Then I slip on a pair of sweatpants and slide into bed beside her.

Emma curls into me like it's natural, like it's right.

And as I hold her sleeping body, her hair tickling my chest, her warm legs tanging with mine, it feels right.

Too fucking right to ignore.

But Emma is too damn good for me.

She's all-class and intoxicating sweetness. She's someone with goals and plans and dreams. I'd never be enough for her.

But what if I was better? More?

What if I pursued my own dreams and cared about things that mattered?

Could I ever deserve her?

"God, I need to drink more." Emma announces as she walks into my living room the next morning.

Chuckling, I place my laptop on the coffee table and

glance up. And my breath freezes in my throat. Because Emma changed. She's no longer wearing the sexy, backless dress from last night. Nope. She's wearing something better. One of my T-shirts. It hits her mid-thigh and is the least sexy thing in the universe. Unless it's covering Emma's body. Because seeing her in one of my boxing T-shirts causes lava to spread through my body and forces me to lean forward, desperate to touch her. "I've never heard anyone say that with a hangover."

"If I didn't take such a hiatus from partying, and drinking, I wouldn't feel like such shit right now." Emma groans, flopping next to me on the couch, her feet swinging into my lap.

"Coffee?"

"And Advil?"

"That too." I agree, squeezing her feet and placing them on the couch. Grabbing the necessities from the kitchen, I return to find Emma sprawled across the entire couch.

"I stole you're shirt."

"Looks better on you."

She grins before squeezing her eyes shut and groaning. "I'm a shit drunk."

"You're hot as shit hungover." I pass her the coffee and tablets.

She takes the pills, washing them down with a large gulp of caffeine. "I'll tell you again; you're a good man, Luke."

I sit on the coffee table and draw my fingers down the side of her face. "What do you need, babe?"

She moves her head the tiniest inch and forces her eyes open. "Netflix binge?"

"I can make that happen."

One side of her mouth lifts into a grin and I lean forward to kiss it.

"I'm starting to like you too much."

"I liked you too much from the start, babe." I flip on the TV and navigate to Netflix. "What are we watching?"

"*Cinderella Man*."

I cut her a look.

"Afterwards, you can call your coach person and tell him you're in."

I raise an eyebrow. "Just like that?"

"I don't think Lone Wolves make decisions they regret, Luke."

I shift her upper body and slide beneath her on the couch. Placing her head in my lap, I run my hand over her silky hair. "Why's that?"

She looks up at me, her eyes filled with compassion. And truth. "Because they have too many regrets to begin with. Otherwise, they'd still be part of a pack."

"I should take the fight."

"You have to take the fight." She wraps her hand around the back of my neck and draws my face to hers, brushing her lips across mine. "No regrets, Luke."

No REGRETS, *Luke.*

Picking up my phone, I punch in the numbers for Scoop.

"Rayes." He answers on the first ring.

"It's Luke. If the offer still stands, I'm in. I want the fight."

He's quiet for several seconds, and my stomach sinks. I'm too late. I should have called him sooner.

"I'm hungry, Scoop."

"How hungry?"

"Fucking starving." The truth rasps out. I look down, focus on my hands. My tatted knuckles stare back at me.

Lone Wolf. I've always been on my own. A self-made loner who fights for what I want, takes what I need to succeed, and never backs down. *When did all that change?* Resolve strengthens my bones, determination sweeps through my limbs. A lone wolf never quits. Quitting would mean death. "I won't let you down."

"Then we better get to work. But, I need one hundred twenty percent from you, Luke. You have to be committed, focused, determined."

"I am."

"Stay starving. For this, you have to stay starving."

"I swear it."

"We start tomorrow. Meet me at The Cellar at 7:00 AM. We'll work out a schedule, your meal plan, targets, all of it. But I'm warning you, I'm tough on my guys, I don't put up with any bullshit, and I don't accept excuses. Ever."

"I understand."

"One hundred and twenty percent."

"See you tomorrow." I end the call.

Leaning my head back against the couch cushions, I drop my phone next to me and curl my hands into fists.

A lone wolf has no regrets.

A lone wolf survives.

12

LUKE

"Lucas." The sound of Uncle P's voice causes my steps to falter. *What the hell does he want now?*

"Uncle P." I step beside him, unlocking the door and holding it open. "What's going on?"

"Shut the door, Lucas," he glares, his blue eyes cold as frost.

I kick the door shut. Turning to face him, I square my shoulders, crossing my arms over my chest. *Why is he here?* Today, of all days. I don't have time for this shit. "Something I can do for you?"

Uncle P sneers at me, his mouth twisting into an ugly line of hate. "I think you should be thinking about everything that I do for you, Lucas, before you take that tone with me again. Who do you think I am? Your mother?"

I fight the urge to spit in his face. Mainly because I owe him so much fucking money. And he's Gray's dad.

His face smooths out once more, his burst of anger reined in. "I haven't seen a change in Grayson. What have you managed to accomplish? I'm practically hemorrhaging money to help your little Cajun hut stay in the black, and you're doing what exactly?" His eyebrows furrow in mock thought, "If I recall correctly, the agreement was I give you money in exchange for your convincing Grayson to stand beside me when I announce my bid for the Presidential nomination, to join me in politics. I need him by my side come January. I need him to accept his rightful place in this city. As a leader. Not as a good-time bartender in a failing business of Cajun cuisine."

My stomach sinks at his reminder. I haven't said anything to Gray about his dad or politics or Uncle P's intention to run for the presidential bid because I find it repugnant. I was hoping to pay Uncle P back before we got to the reminder phase of our agreement. I don't want to screw Gray over. I don't want to persuade him to do something he doesn't want to just because his dad's a dick.

Keeping my face smooth, I lie. "I am talking to Gray. It's not my fault he doesn't want to pursue politics."

"I highly doubt that, Lucas. I think you're stalling. I know you're not fulfilling your end of our arrangement. In fact, I think you lack the necessary motivation to do so."

I raise my eyebrows, but my stomach falls to the floor.

"I'm willing to overlook your lack of commitment if you drop out of the fight against Joe Carney."

How did Uncle P find out about the fight? "What the hell does that have to do with anything?"

He sighs as if I'm wasting his time. "Lucas, I have many business interests in this city. Surely you recognize that?"

I nod.

"Joe Carney is a cash cow. He could have easily destroyed Nova, even with his doping. You?" He shakes his head, "You I'm not so sure about, and I need the cow to keep producing milk. Do you understand?"

A bubble of irrational laughter works its way out of my

throat. "Are you kidding me? You want me to back down from the chance of a lifetime, because you don't want to miss out on some extra cash? Uncle P, this is my dream. I can't let this go. I have to take this fight."

"Dreams are for artists and other wayward souls. I'm not interested in your dreams, Lucas. Harrington's don't dream. We do. And we do by having the necessary status, prestige, and wealth to make things happen. Back out of the fight."

"No." I step closer, my frame looming over him. "I'm not dropping the fight. Our agreement was for Gray and me to stand by you and I'm still willing to do that, to talk to Gray. But there's no way in hell I'm dropping out of this fight. Not for you. Not for anyone."

He glowers at me, anger reddening his neck before he takes a deep breath. "Very well. In that case, I'll need to provide you with the necessary motivation to honor your original commitments, which you're failing to do. Ten thousand dollars, Lucas. Due to me by next weekend. Or I tell Gray all about your little plan to manipulate him in exchange for money. Like a common whore." He smiles now, and strangely enough, it looks real. He's getting a kick out of this. Out of extorting his own nephew. He nods then, as if it's settled. "I look forward to receiving your payment in full."

Then he's gone, the ding of the elevator the only sound in the hallway.

I blow out a shaky breath and fight the urge to put my fist through the wall.

ME: *Hey, can you close tonight?*
  Gray: *OK, all good?*
  Me: *Yeah, something came up.*

Gray: ??

Me: Walk Emma to metro.

Gray: Duh.

I've procrastinated for hours, my head filled with thoughts about how to come up with Uncle P's money. I hate the unknown that looms over me like a thundercloud if I blow Uncle P off. *Would he out me to Gray? Would he go after Barracuda? Would he send a bunch of thugs to rattle me?*

And, if I do pay him the money, then what?

Will he up the ante next weekend? Or next time I piss him off? Or whenever he feels like Gray isn't responding the way he wants him to?

How do I come up with $10,000 in a week? If I had that kind of money, I wouldn't have borrowed it from him in the first place.

Damn. I know how to come up with fast cash. I've been doing it for years. But now, I don't want to blow shit with Scoop. I'm grateful for the opportunity to train with him, to have a shot against Lightning in December. That's only two months from now. I can't risk it all by going underground for a night.

When Scoop finds out, will he drop me?

Dropping my face into my hands, I scrub my eyes.

Think, Luke. What are your main priorities?

Mom's face drifts into my mind; I can't let her down. I can't risk the restaurant and risk her spiraling into a depression so deep it will suck her out of my life like a black hole. I need to keep things going with Barracuda and right now, I need Uncle P's money to do that.

Picking my phone up, I tap out a message to Toby. I know for now he'll keep his mouth shut. Not because he's loyal or anything like that, but because he wants to get paid. He knows I'll flip him extra for being discreet.

An hour later I receive his response.

Toby: Good news. Tonight. Jersey City, NJ. 11PM. Don't be late. I'll text you the address once it's finalized.

Slamming the bottom of my fist against the kitchen cabinet, I breathe a mixture of relief and regret. Relief because I know how to get the money to Uncle P. Regret because I'm not yet sure what it's going to cost me.

I take a quick shower, letting the hot water mute all thoughts for a few moments. Wrapping a towel around my waist, I toss some gear into a duffel bag. I pull on a pair of sweats and a T-shirt, step into a pair of sneakers, and tug a hoodie over my head. Fifteen minutes later, I'm merging onto the Baltimore-Washington Parkway, headed to New Jersey.

THE SMELL of gasoline and antifreeze greet me when I push open the door to the garage.

Lui, the guy who owns it, is nowhere to be seen, but his kid Sonny is sitting on a milk crate out front, watching for cops. I haven't been here before, but I know Lui; most guys do.

Toby texted me the address of the garage as I was crossing into Delaware. A brief glimpse of Emma as a kid flashed through my mind. She mentioned she was from Delaware. I wondered where she had grown up, what high school she attended, if her family was sitting around a dinner table, saying grace, ready to eat the pork chops her mom cooked. For some reason, even though I don't know much about her, about her family, I could envision her upbringing with perfect clarity.

Then I crossed into Jersey, and all thoughts of Emma ceased to exist. I had to focus on the fight.

"You made it," a beefy guy with a neck tattoo that reads "Jasmine" says. I don't recognize him, but it's obvious he knows who I am. They've been expecting me.

"Yeah."

"You can drop your shit there." He points to the corner of the room where there's about a foot of space between the wall and a red Snap-On Industrial tool set. I walk over, toss my duffel bag in the corner, and turn to survey the group.

There are twelve guys present, each dressed casually in sweats, jeans, and hoodies. Every one of them is wearing an unreadable expression. They're all jacked as shit. A few girls walk in and out, bringing the guys beers, cigarettes, an ass to slap.

For a moment, I consider the possibility that this is a set up and they're going to pounce on me and knock me out until I'm half-dead but then I remember that this is Lui's garage. And with Lui, money is always changing hands.

"You're fighting, Keys." Neck Tattoo says, pointing to a tall guy with a chinstrap who's built like a linebacker.

I fight the urge to smile; I nod instead.

"Yous should both know the rules." Man, this guy is straight Jersey. "In case you forgot, I'll run through 'em real quick. No eye gouging, no kicking, no biting. You want to wrap your hands; you do the lower half and wrist only. This is bare-knuckles. You get knocked out, you're done. Otherwise, yous keep going. Any questions?"

"What's the purse?" Keys asks, a glint in his eye.

"Forty large," Sonny speaks up.

Keys and I retreat to our corners of the garage to mentally prepare, wrap the portions of our hands that are allowed, and grab some water. I pop a mouth guard in.

Keys and I meet in the center of the garage which the guys have designated the "ring." We bump fists. Neck Tattoo drops a white bandana, signaling the start of the fight. Keys stares me down hard, but I keep my face blank. We circle each other. Once. Twice. And then he starts to jab. *One, two. One, two, cross.*

I keep my feet moving. Lean away from his punches. Keep my hands up to guard my face.

I jab quick. *One, two. One, two, hook.*

Catching him under the jaw, his face snaps to the left. I follow it up with an undercut, knocking his head back.

A few cheers ring out.

Keys' eyes flash, a bloodthirsty hardness I'm familiar with. His jabs are controlled, his footwork solid. He's not an amateur. He must need this money just as badly as I do.

He throws another punch, landing it on my jaw, right under my left ear. Pain sears through the side of my head before he lands another jab, splitting the skin under my right eye. Fuck, it burns. I feel the heat of my blood dripping down my face, but I don't pause. We've felt each other out, sized each other up, and we both know this is going to be one hell of a fight. But it's not going to end until one of us is down.

And it needs to be him.

WHEN I CLIMB into my car at 1:00 AM, I swear I'm half-dead.

I know I shouldn't be driving. I know I need to pull over and crash somewhere for a few hours. Maybe in one of those random rest stops that always have vending machines with stale cookies. I should at least pass through a McDonald's for a coffee. But once I'm on the I-95, I keep going, watching the various mile markers and exit signs, knowing I am that much closer to home.

My body aches everywhere. I feel my heartbeat in my temples, under my right eye, in my jaw. I'm sure my nose is broken. I've got a split lip, a busted jaw, and my right eyelid is hanging so low I can barely see out of my eye.

Everything hurts. Even breathing.

Emma: Hey, all okay? Gray says he's closing for you tonight.

Emma: Luke, you need anything?

Ah, my sweet girl. I should message her; I don't want her to worry.

But what the hell do I say?

I fought an illegal bout and won a cool $40,000? A grin cuts my face. What a fucking relief.

I flipped $15,000 to Toby as a thank you for setting up the fight. It's more than his usual $10,000 but the extra 5K is an incentive to keep his mouth shut. Scoop is going to tear into me, and I don't need all the other guys finding out about this.

Now I can toss $10,000 to Uncle P. I know I can pick up some more underground fights and make back all the money I owe him, but then I'll never have the opportunity to go pro. And no one will ever want to come into my restaurant if I look like I got jumped in a back alley somewhere shady and need a freaking Tetanus shot.

Fuck. I hurt.

Two more hours to go.

THE NIGHT SKY is lightening in varying degrees of blue and purple when I pull into a parking spot in front of Barracuda around 4 AM. I know I should go home, but I'm nervous walking around with all this cash. I want to dump it in the safe here where I know it will be secure. Well, more so than at my apartment with the shitty lock.

I unlock the door to the restaurant, making sure to flip the lock behind me, and limp into the office. Depositing the paper bag stacked with bills in my safe, I lock it and literally collapse on the couch in the corner. Too exhausted to move, too sore to try, I close my eyes and let an image of Emma's face block out daybreak.

13

EMMA

A n irritating sound penetrates my subconscious… effectively interrupting a moment between Luke and me.

Luke and I kissing under a blanket of stars on a beautiful, quiet beach in… Greece.

Ring, ring, ring.

Opening my eyes from my sensual dream, I am so, so tempted to throw my stupid phone across the room and slip back into the delicious dream.

Shoving the phone under my pillow, I close my eyes again.

Recalling Luke's tight abs, the way his tattoos curl around his wrists and over his knuckles, the stubble that covers his cheeks and chin, I imagine the breeze whispering along the beach, the scent of sea and darkness.

His rough hands come up to frame my face, his fingers lacing in my hair, anchoring my forehead against his as he looks into my eyes. Longingly.

I sigh, my gaze skimming over his lips, my fingers itching to touch him. Reaching up slowly, I –

Ring, ring, ring.

You've got to be kidding me.

My eyes pop open, met with the darkness of my bedroom, the beach in Greece already fading from memory.

Freaking alarm.

I turn it off before the incessant sound wakes Cassie. Stuffing my face into my pillow, I whine to myself for a few moments, forcing myself to move past the interruption of my imaginary, subconsciously hopeful, lovefest with a guy who looks like a Greek god.

No chance of drifting back to a peaceful sleep now, I drag myself from bed.

Checking my phone, my stomach dips that there's no waiting message from Luke.

Is he okay? Why hasn't he responded to my messages?

Oh my God, stop being so clingy!

Not clingy, concerned.

See, this is why you can't casually date? You suck at casual!

Just get up and get in the office. Meet your goals.

Yes, goals I wrote down just last night in pink pen in my pretty, shimmery, Kate Spade planner. I need to be in the office early, fulfill my responsibilities, and use the extra time to create my own initiative, demonstrate to the team, to Senator LeBeau, that I am a valuable asset. Who wouldn't want to hire Emma Stanton?

Stretching my arms overhead, I block my analysis of Luke's lack of text messages from my mind. Flipping through the hangers in my closet, I settle on a simple navy dress with cap sleeves that hits just below my knee. I clasp a thin hot pink belt around my waist for flare and step into nude pumps. Fixing my hair and makeup, I grab my nude purse and peek inside to make sure I have all the essentials: wallet, ID, sweater, phone, planner, makeup bag.

Shoot, no keys.

Where are my keys?

Barracuda! I left them on Luke's desk when I was helping Gray close last night.

Glancing at my watch, an old Rolex that belonged to my mother, I'm thankful for my newfound status as early-morning riser because I have time to swing by Barracuda and pick up my keys. I need them to get into Senator LeBeau's office. Plus, the cleaning crew is usually at Barracuda by now, mopping the sticky floors and wiping down the even stickier bar.

Grabbing a banana from the fruit bowl on the kitchen counter, I pick my trench up off the back of the couch, and close the door behind me, thankful it locks automatically.

Waiting for the elevator, I pull my phone out of my purse and glance at the screen for news and updates.

Newsworthy Headlines:

Twitter: (Incredibly delicious photo of an ice cream cone with THREE scoops of gelato) For you @EmmaStanton #gelateria #WhenInRome #fragola #pistacchio #cioccolato

I laugh at Mia's tweet. It's good to receive visual confirmation that she's enjoying Rome... and eating up all the goodness the city has to offer. Sure, we have some good ice cream here in the U.S., but nothing comes close to Italian gelato.

Ding. I step into the elevator as the doors open and continue scrolling.

Lila posted a Facebook picture of her and hottie-with-the-body Cade Wilkins leaning over to kiss her cheek affection-ately. It's so cute, it's gross.

The air is chilly this morning and I shrug into my trench coat, cinching the belt around my waist. There's a Starbucks on nearly every corner as I walk from the metro stop down Eighth Street. Popping into one, I order a grande nonfat latte before continuing on to Barracuda.

A beat-up Blazer is parked out front.

What's Luke doing here so early?

What the hell?

He couldn't message me because he was...here?

Stop, Emma. I'm sure there's a good reason.

And, now you can definitely grab your keys.

Trying the front door, I frown that it's locked. I knock a few times, rocking from foot to foot.

Peering around the door, I peek into the window in time to see a disheveled Luke staggering out of the back office.

Oh my God. Is he drunk?

Swaying uncertainly, he reaches out to settle himself on a nearby table and squints his eyes at me.

Holy guacamole.

My breath lodges in my throat as I take in his appearance. He looks like he got the shit kicked out of him. I bang my open palm against the window, securing his attention with my sudden urgency.

What the hell happened?

He should be in a hospital.

Why didn't he message me?

Eternity passes before the front door swings open.

"Luke, are you okay?" I step into the restaurant and wrap a hand around his wrist. Guiding him to a nearby table, I push him into a chair. "What happened?"

Slowly, he raises his head.

"Oh my God."

His right eye is swollen completely closed. He has dried blood caked around his mouth and the right side of his nose. The entire left side of his face is covered in a mottle of blue and purple bruises.

"Shoulda seen the other guy." He wheezes.

"Luke," I whisper-breathe. Trailing my fingers from his wrist over his hand, he winces and I look down. "Jesus." I take in his knuckles, split, cracked, and caked with bloody scabs. "What happened?"

"Don't worry about it. I'm fine."

I'm so caught off guard by his blasé response that I don't even try to hide my surprise. "Fine? You look like you've been attacked by a mountain lion."

He chuckles but his face contorts in pain, and he grimaces instead. "Don't make me laugh."

"I'm not trying to. I'm not even funny."

"Yes, you are. But only when you're not trying to be."

"Luke, please, tell me what happened. Are you in trouble?"

"No, Emma, I'm really great." He says this seriously and I squint at him, my concern growing with each sentence he utters.

"Did you hit your head?" I lean in, my hands cupping his cheeks.

"What are you doing?"

"Checking your pupils. You're clearly concussed."

He shakes his head, his hands reaching up and locking on my wrists. "I'm not."

"How do you know? I highly doubt that you went to a hospital last night."

He tugs my wrists and I step closer to him, standing between his thighs.

"Trust me, Emma. I'm fine. This is nothing. What are you doing here this early?"

This is nothing? Does he mean he's been beaten worse than this before? "Stop trying to change the subject."

"If I tell you the truth, will you let it go?"

"Will you tell me honestly if you need a doctor?"

"I don't."

Huffing again, I take a minuscule step closer, enjoying the heat from his body as his thighs tighten around mine. "Fine. What happened?"

"I had a fight last night."

"You had a fight last night." I repeat. As usual. "For boxing?"

He nods.

"I'm not buying it." I shake my head. "Boxers have a few cuts and bruises. They don't look like, like, this," I gesture up-and-down his body. "If this is how you look after a fight, how come I've never seen you like this before?" I wonder aloud although my mind is already flipping through memories. Memories of Luke looking tired, hunching his shoulders, protecting one side of his body, sporting random bruises. Come to think of it, there have been times when I've questioned why he holds himself in a certain position. Maybe he is telling the truth.

"Because I normally don't do bare-knuckles. Anymore."

"You fought with no gloves or pads or whatever the protective equipment is called?" I shout, frustration for his carelessness erupting out of me. "I thought you quit that!"

He winces at the sudden volume of my voice and I almost feel bad. Almost.

He nods again.

"Is that even legal?"

He smiles now, a little uptick to the left side of his mouth. "Sometimes."

I snort, reading between the lines. "That means last night wasn't legal."

"I told you the truth. I had a fight last night. That's it. And before you ask again, I'm fine. Now, why are you here so early?"

I study him for another beat. He seems fine; he's acting like his moody, unreadable self. "I forgot my keys."

"Where?"

"On your desk."

He drops my wrists and pushes himself up to standing, using the table as leverage. "I'll go grab them for you."

"Please stop." I place a hand in the center of his chest. "I can get them." I try to sidestep him but he waves me off, limping away and disappearing into his office.

A few moments later, Luke stands before me, my key ring looped around his index finger. He drops the keys into my open palm. "Don't worry about me, babe. I'm really okay."

"Will you call me if you need anything? Like for real?"

"Sure. I like your dress."

I look down, smoothing my palms over the material clinging to my thighs. "Really?"

"You look very professional."

"Well, that's a relief since that's the look I'm going for."

"And very beautiful." He reaches out, twirling a lock of my hair around his finger.

"Thank you." I whisper, turning into his touch.

"Have a good day, babe." He presses a kiss to my forehead and my eyes flutter closed.

I breathe in his spicy cologne and fresh soap and something so masculine it makes my mouth water.

"What time do you have to be at work?"

Right. I need to go to work. "I need to get going. See you later?"

"Yeah, Em."

"Promise you're okay?"

"Swear it. I'm better than okay."

"This is a joke, right? You're pulling my chain, Luke? Because I don't ever remember picking up a fighter to train and then have him take an underground fight, get the shit beat out of him, and chance ruining everything we're building here at the gym. What the hell were you thinking?"

What if Scoop drops me? What if I just fucked up my own dream?

"I'm sorry Scoop. I really am. It won't happen again."

"Damn right it won't. I swear Luke, another guy pulls a stunt like this, I would drop him. No questions asked. But we're too damn close to the fight and there's too much riding on this." He sighs, rubbing a palm over his shaved head. "You really messed up. And I don't think you understand the gravity of it because there's barely a consequence." He shakes his head, muttering to himself. He tosses out a few more curses and reprimands.

I keep my mouth shut tight because though I often act like an idiot, even I know when it's time to stay silent.

Scoop snaps his fingers suddenly. "Have you ever been paid to fight?"

I stare at him.

"Not underground. But in a sanctioned fight?"

I shake my head.

"Okay. We need to rectify that immediately. I'll pull it together for tomorrow morning. Go home and get some rest. You look like shit. Ice your face. Tomorrow you take your status from amateur to professional. And I hope the guy puts up a tough fight because I'm still pissed as hell with you. But we gotta job to do."

I stand slowly, my entire body aching. A fight tomorrow? With the shape I'm in, it seems impossible. "Thank you, Scoop. Really."

He shakes his head at me again, taking in my stooped-over stance and disappointment colors his eyes and his words. "Step up to the plate, kid. I didn't tag you for this type of bullshit."

Remorse settles around my shoulders at his words because I know he's right. I did it again. I let Uncle P get to me and I caved, giving into his demands as usual. "It won't happen again."

"Better not, Harrington." I wince at the sound of my last name. I loved my Dad, really loved him. And I love Gray, he's my brother. But every time I hear my last name I feel a connection to my uncle which always leaves me feeling defensive and unsettled. Talk about a chip on a shoulder.

I exhale through my lips and nod once at Scoop before limping past him to exit the gym.

"I'll message you the details for tomorrow's fight. Be first, Luke. I swear to God you need to show me something real tomorrow because I'm starting to wonder why the hell I'm bothering with you."

I nod again, meeting his gaze one last time before going home and collapsing on my bed.

I sleep for nine hours.

SCOOP'S MESSAGE the next morning has me in knots.

Today is the day I become a pro boxer.

The fight is at 2:00 PM at a nearby gym. All I know is that I'm fighting a local guy who's been around for ages and knows the ins and outs of the industry. The fight has been approved by one of the sanctioning bodies. I have no clue how Scoop managed to pull this off so quickly, the entire thing is unheard of. But then again, he's Scoop "Hurricane" Rayes. I guess he has some pull somewhere.

I pull into the parking lot at 1:30 PM and take a few minutes to get my head straight. *This is it.* This is the first step to having a real career. Taking a steadying breath, I'm about to shoulder my gym bag and exit the Blazer when my phone dings from the center console with a text.

Emma: Hey, hope your face is healing. Good luck today. Make sure you don't get hit. For real. I'd hate to see you look like a rainbow forever. (Winking emoji, rainbow emoji)

I grin. Only Emma would send me an emoji of a rainbow, hell any emoji, and it would result in a smile. Taking her message as a sign of good luck to come, I drop my phone back in the center console and make my way into the gym.

I'm not sure what to expect when I walk through the double doors, but a legit boxing gym unfolds around me. Scoop is standing next to the ring, talking with Cliff from The Cellar. He raises an arm when he spots me and I walk over to them.

"You ready?" he asks me, his voice hard.

I nod.

Cliff gives me a look out of the corner of his eye. By now,

everyone has heard about the underground fight, and I know all the guys think I'm a jackass. Who gets so close to a one-in-a-million opportunity and nearly blows it all to get beat up in a garage in North Jersey? It sounds stupid to myself when I think about it like that.

"I'm ready," I say after both guys spend two beats too long studying me. I'm sore as hell. My face is a canvas of mottled colors: blue, black, purple, and yellow. I can hear my breath wheeze in and out like a whisper when I breathe. But damn it all, I'm ready for this.

"You're fighting Simon Duarte," Cliff throws out.

"The Snake?" I ask, surprised. I didn't realize I would fight someone so well known for this.

Cliff nods.

"Suit up," Scoop demands, turning back to Cliff, ignoring me.

I wrap my hands and spend some time warming up.

At 2:00 PM, Simon and I climb into the ring. Some of the other guys around the gym have wandered over to watch. An official referee goes through the rules and tells us the purse is $200. Simon smiles at this and cuts his eyes to me. He's a nice guy. I'm sure he's using today as a workout while for me, today changes everything. It marks a new chapter in my life.

The bell rings, and I watch Simon with precision-like focus. Every jab I throw today will be clean, every combination crisp. We circle each other slowly, pawing with jabs that feel each other out. In round three, I lay into him with a series of combinations that catch him off-guard. From that moment on, the two of us engage in full-out boxing. We're evenly matched in height and weight, and while Simon has more experience than me, I have more stamina. We keep at it for eight rounds before the decision goes to the cards to decide who won. I stand in my corner, hunched over and wheezing, trying to catch my breath as Scoop pours water over the top of my head.

"You did a hell of a job, kid."

The referee steps to the center of the ring after collecting the cards from the three judges present. Simon and I step forward, waiting for the winner to be announced.

The referee glances at the card in his hand and eyes Simon and me before announcing, "By split decision, the winner of the bout is… Luke Harrington." The ref raises my arm over my head as the guys in the gym whistle and clap.

I almost crumple to my knees in relief and surprise. As desperately as I wanted to win this, hoped I pulled it off, I wasn't sure I had it. Simon is a formidable fighter and kept me on my toes the entire match.

Simon throws an arm around my shoulders. "Congratulations, Luke. You earned this. Welcome to boxing." He taps the back of my neck as the referee hands me $200.

"Thanks man."

"Good luck in December." He slaps my back again and pushes me toward Scoop and Cliff.

"Good fight, Luke." Scoop says when I make it back to my corner.

"Thanks Scoop. For everything."

He nods, placing a hand on my shoulder and squeezing. "You earned this. Now don't muck the rest of it up."

"Stay starving."

"Exactly."

For the first time in a long time, an actual laugh works its way out of my mouth.

Holy shit, I'm a professional boxer.

15

EMMA

L uke's face is healing nicely.

A lot nicer than my face would heal if I got beat up like that. While I'm positive I'd look deranged, he somehow looks hotter. Edgier. Sexier.

How is that even possible when I want him the way I do?

Clearing off a table, I stack the dirty plates in a black bin and hug it to my hip as I make my rounds, scraping food from dirty dishes, organizing cutlery, stacking glasses, shutting down Barracuda for the night. My bangs fall into my eyes and small drops of sweat bead on my forehead. I'm exhausted. So tired that the muscles in my back don't even ache anymore, they're just numb.

Is Luke coming in tonight?

Luke and I are doing one hell of a confusing dance.

We flirt. We kiss. We talk.

I slept in his bed.

But I have absolutely no idea where I stand with him.

Are we dating? Hooking up? Just friends?

The entire thing is puzzling and yet, when I'm with him, I'm relaxed and comfortable. Being with Luke is nothing like being with Josh McCannon. There's no awkwardness, no trying to be someone I'm not, no worrying about sucking in my stomach when I sit or stressing over which dress makes me look the slimmest. I'm just...me. And that's enough for him.

And yet, we still haven't really hooked up.

Truth, it's not from my lack of trying.

Whenever Luke sees me, his face brightens. Whenever he kisses me, his eyes close almost as if I'm causing him pain. The man confuses the hell out of me and yet, I crave him.

I dream about him.

I think of him all the time.

Like right now.

Gah! The entire thing is unhealthy. Like an addiction.

"Emma?"

I jump, twirling around.

"I didn't mean to scare you, babe." Luke shadows the doorframe, a key set in his hand.

Clutching my chest, I drop the black bin on a nearby table and shake my head. "Hey. No, it's okay. I just wasn't expecting anyone."

"I'm surprised you're still here."

"Just cleaning up," I gesture to the mess piled around me.

A crease settles between Luke's eyebrows, marking his face with the scowl I'm starting to adore. Although, upon further examination, I'm beginning to realize there are several variations to Luke's scowl. Little nuances that make all the difference. For example, the crease between his eyebrows hints at confusion, the small twist of his lips is for amusement, and the downward tug of his eyebrows is a combination of frustration and concern. Context clues necessary to decipher that one. All of this with a scowl. Alas, maybe I just stare at him too much.

I totally do.

"Where's Gray?"

"He had an emergency." I add another stack of plates to the bin.

"An emergency? Did he say what?" His eyebrows draw together before dipping downward. I'm going with concern on this one.

"Something about his dad."

"You're alone?" he asks, realization finally dawning that yes, indeed, zero-experience Emma Stanton is commanding the restaurant tonight.

"Yeah. But don't worry, I went over all the checklists. Everything went pretty well. I mean, I still have to close out the register so, fingers crossed, nothing is off, but otherwise, it was a steady night. Raoul and Hector were super supportive and –" *Oh my God, stop rambling.* "It was fine, really, I know things may seem an utter disaster in this moment but …" I trail off when his eyes cut to me, blazing green.

"Babe, what the hell? Why didn't you call me?" He steps forward, curling a hand around my upper arm. "You okay?"

"Me? Yeah, I'm fine." I blow out a breath, enjoying the cool breeze as it ruffles my bangs away from my forehead. I'm really sweating now. *Because that's attractive.* "And I know how busy you are with your new training schedule."

Luke shakes his head, his eyes scanning the disaster around us. Nearly every table is dirty. I've barely had time to clear tables in between customers sitting at them. Now that the restaurant is closed, well, I'm working my way through the mess one table at a time.

"Where are Hector and Raoul?"

"They had to leave. They didn't want to." I hurry to reassure him that they didn't abandon me as his scowl deepens. "I made them go. You know Raoul has to catch the bus back to

Virginia. If he misses it, he'll be waiting for hours at the station and it'll be really difficult for his family since he's the one who stops by his grandmas to give her medicine." *Stop rambling.* "And Hector's daughter came down with a fever. He was so worried; I couldn't let him... I'm fine, Luke, really." I imagine I look like a sweating pig ripe for slaughter trying to talk my way out of it. Like Wilbur.

"Jesus, babe. This is a lot of fucking work. I had no idea you were here on your own or I would have come to help you."

"It's really okay. You need to focus on your fight. Your dream."

"Babe, let's finish this and go for dinner. You must be starving."

"I really am."

Luke chuckles, picking up the bin. "I've got this. Why don't you restock the bar?"

"Okay." Stepping behind the bar, I begin restocking the cocktail napkins and straws, emptying the fruit trays, draining the ice chest. Focused on my work and letting my mind go blank, I'm surprised when Luke knocks on top of the bar, gaining my attention.

"Almost done?"

I look around. Barracuda is restored to its usual neatness. "You're finished?"

"I haven't spent the last six hours running around, plating food, chatting with customers, and smiling the entire time."

"How do you know I smiled the entire time?"

"Because you're always smiling." He swipes his thumb over my cheekbone, hooking his hand around the back of my neck. "Just seeing you makes me happy." He pulls me forward and presses a hard kiss to my mouth.

"I'm seriously disgusting." I murmur against his lips.

"You're seriously perfect." He nips my bottom lip and squeezes the back of my neck. "What are you in the mood for? Steak, Italian, sushi?"

"Italian."

"I can do Italian. Come on."

"Just give me a second to not look like such a hot mess." I glance down at my sweaty T-shirt and stained black jeans.

"Take all the time you want but babe, you always look hot."

"Forget your wallet?" I joke thirty minutes later as the elevator dings to the floor of his apartment.

Luke chuckles, unlocking his door and guiding me inside. "Em, nothing's open this late. So, I'm cooking dinner."

"Seriously?" I twist to look at him.

"I can do Italian." He swats my ass. "Make yourself comfortable."

"Bet you're relieved I didn't say sushi, huh?"

"You have no idea."

Slipping onto one of the barstools at his kitchen island, I watch as he sets up his workspace. "Need help?"

"Nervous I can't boil water?" He winks, pulling out a cutting board. "I do own a restaurant, you know?"

"Yeah, and yet I've never seen you so much as pick up a knife."

"True. I'm not much of a cook but I can do a few basics. Red okay?" He picks up a wine bottle.

"Perfect; I need a glass of wine."

"Being on your own at the restaurant isn't easy." He agrees, pouring me a generous glass.

"What? You're not drinking?" I ask as he corks the bottle.

"Nah. Training." He begins to chop garlic and tomatoes.

"How's it going?"

"Brutal. But I'd only admit that to you. Scoop is kicking my ass but I need it."

"Are you worried about the fight?" I ask, sipping the wine. Some of the tension in my shoulders dissipates as the first sip travels through my body, warming my blood.

"A little." He admits, glancing over at me. His expression wary, his eyes flashing. "What if I'm not good enough?"

"To beat this Lightning guy?"

Luke's lips twist as he focuses back on the cutting board, a sharp staccato ringing out. "Yeah. I keep thinking about why I didn't jump at the chance to take the fight. Was it really Barracuda and Uncle Steve's legacy and Mom? Or was that all some bullshit excuse because deep down, I'm fucking terrified I'm going to get my shot and blow the whole thing."

"Hey. Don't do that."

"What?"

"Second guess yourself like that. The moment you make room for doubt is the moment you give up control."

"Did you read that on a motivational poster?"

"I'm serious! And surprised."

"Huh?" He stops chopping and shifts forward. "Why surprised?"

"You seem like a guy who likes to be in control."

"I do." He nearly growls, his eyes darkening.

"So why are you giving it away to these stupid, distracting thoughts?"

"I'm not. I'm just confiding in you that —"

"You're good enough, Luke. You're even better."

"You don't know anything about this. You don't know Lightning."

"I know you." I take another sip of the wine, placing the

glass down and standing on the rung of the barstool. Clasping his face between my hands, I admit, "I see you, Luke. You think you're lost and drowning. You think you're confused and questioning if you're making the right decision. But all I see is a man doing right by everyone else. You're scared that if you take this shot for yourself and don't succeed then you let everyone down. But Luke, you're going to win. Not because you're the better fighter, which I think you are, but because you're the better man. And you want this. You told me yourself you have to stay starving. I see you starving. And working. And busting your ass to do everything right. Don't doubt yourself."

He freezes, his entire being locking down. But his eyes, his beautiful, bright green eyes, flare to life. Heat licks at his irises, building into a flame even as his lips press into a thin line. "You really believe that?"

"I do."

He clears his throat, shaking off my touch. "You're too good for me, Emma."

Grinning, I take another sip of my wine. "With an attitude like that, you'll win my dad over no problem."

Luke snickers, alleviating some of the tension in the room. "Meeting the parents already?"

"Oh, it will happen eventually, Luke."

Stirring pasta at the stove, he glances at me over his shoulder. "I'm not really the type of guy you bring home to daddy."

"That's part of the problem."

"What is?"

"You don't really know what type of guy you are."

Luke sighs, draining the pasta and fixing two plates. "I wish I saw me the way you do, babe."

"That's something I definitely understand." I agree,

wishing I could see myself the way he seems too. Tipping back my wine glass, I enjoy the bold red.

Luke slides a plate piled with penne in a light tomato sauce topped with basil and pecorino-romano cheese in front of me. I want to face plant into its aromatic goodness. My stomach growls, and if I wasn't literally starving, there's a chance I would be embarrassed. Maybe.

"Now, let's be serious. This looks amazing." I pick up my fork.

Luke chuckles, spearing some penne with his fork. "*Bon appétit.*"

But I'm already chewing. The sauce is light and sweet with a hint of garlic and basil. The pasta is perfectly al dente. Oh my God, I'm in food heaven.

"Thank you," I tell Luke in between bites. "Really, I haven't had a home-cooked meal in so long I can't even – actually, it was the morning I left for my internship. My dad made me pancakes." I shovel another forkful into my mouth. Happiness.

After another two bites and a gulp of wine, I feel Luke staring at me. Turning toward him, I drop my fork to wipe my napkin across my mouth, suddenly mortified that I have sauce smeared across my face but don't realize it because I'm too focused on the delicious tastes exploding in my mouth.

"Do I have food all over my face?"

"I like watching you eat. It's fascinating."

"You mean it's like watching a lion kill an antelope." I supply, returning my fork to my dish. "I'm sorry." I glance down as heat blossoms in my cheeks. It's bad enough that I'm bigger than other girls, but do I really have to act like it too? Draw attention to the fact that I'll never be a size two? Or four? Or six? Or –

"Don't ever be sorry, babe." Luke brushes my hair out of

my eyes and grips my chin, forcing me to look at him. His other hand palms my thigh, rooting me to the barstool, and stealing the breath from my lungs. "Don't ever change, Emma. It's a relief to see a woman actually enjoy her food, appreciate the flavors, eat without counting the calories or carbs or whatever the hell it is women do to obsess about their weight." And with that statement, he hits the nail right on the head. *How did he know that I'm sitting here, secretly obsessing?* "You're beautiful the way you are. I'm serious, don't change."

"Thank you." I spear two more pieces of penne onto the tines of my fork.

"No, Emma. Thank you." Luke's deep green eyes sear in their intensity. "For everything."

16

LUKE

E mma smacks her lips and I swear, I want to be the piece of pasta that she bites into. I've never seen anyone eat the way she does, appreciating every bite, breathing in the garlic and basil, her eyes closing as a sigh falls from her lips. Emma eats sensually.

And it's fucking hot.

I scoop another heaving spoonful of penne onto her plate, wanting her to keep eating just so I can watch her, hear the sweet moans of pleasure that drop from her lips. I swear, I would cook for her every night of my life if this was the reaction it would produce.

And the worst part is, I can imagine it.

Emma walking into a beautiful kitchen, toeing off her heels, and sliding onto a barstool. Me, stirring a pot at the stove, passing her a wine glass. She'd uncork a bottle of Merlot, her bright smile peeking behind her wine glass as she takes a sip and tells me about her day.

Thoughts like these, that hint at the future, are so far-fetched that even dreaming them up causes a pang of regret for what will never be to ache in my chest.

Whatever is happening between Emma and me is temporary at best and probably better never explored. Because women like her, women who appreciate pasta dinners and take on extra responsibilities because the guys she works with have their own family struggles to handle, the ones who stay late and don't call you for help, are way too fucking good for a wannabe boxer with no formal education to fall back on.

Emma deserves more than I could ever give her, so why even go there?

She slides off the barstool, picking up my empty plate and stacking it on top of hers as she rounds the counter to enter the kitchen.

"What are you doing?" I jump up.

"You cooked, I clean."

"Get out of here." I take the dishes from her hand, dropping them into the sink. I stick my hip out, boxing her out from getting near the sink. "You're at my house, I'll do the dishes."

"No way! That's not how the rule goes."

"What rule?

"You cooked. I clean. Fair and square."

"This isn't playground rules. Fair and square," I mimic her, laughing as she struggles to move around me. Her sweet little body is pressed up against my back as she attempts to cut around my right side. I block her easily.

"Hey!" she protests.

I'm not prepared when her fingers shoot out and tickle me. Holy fuck. Something most people don't know about me is that I am ticklish as hell. Nothing brings me to my knees faster. I falter, laughing unexpectedly, trying to swat her hands away from their path around my ribcage.

"Stop!" I grab her wrist and raise our joined hands in the

air as she ducks under my arm and comes at me with her other hand.

"I can't believe you're ticklish!" she squeals, her voice filled with wonder and delight, like a little kid discovering a secret. "Say mercy!"

"Hell no." I dip my right shoulder into her frame and lift her so that her body hangs over my shoulder like a sack of potatoes. "What are you going to do now?" I taunt her, standing to my full height and walking into the living room as she pounds on my back with her fists.

"Put me down!"

"Say mercy."

"Never!"

Stalking into my bedroom, I toss her onto my bed where she lands with an oomph. She raises her hands to ward off my assault and finally shrieks, "Okay, fine, mercy! You win!" She's laughing, embracing the sweet innocence she shares with the world.

I've never met someone so confident in their vulnerability. I want to protect that. Protect her. For as long as I can, anyway. I fall on top of her, caging her in with my forearms. "I always win," I say quietly. "Remember that." It sounds more like a warning than I intend, and her big blue eyes grow serious.

"Okay," she whispers, her breath brushing against my lips.

We're so close that all I have to do is lean down and I can taste her sweet skin.

She's looking up at me, her blue eyes wide and bright and so fucking trusting that it nearly stops me from dipping my mouth closer to hers. The space between us crackles. We both know that once we cross this line, there's no going back.

Because I'm not stopping at a simple kiss and cuddle. And hell, I don't think she wants me to.

I've always taken whatever I wanted. And as much as I want to protect her from everyone else, I want her for myself.

Dropping my mouth, I capture her lips. Sweet, slow, and sensual turns into hot and frenzied in a nanosecond. Emma's skin tastes like peaches and summertime and I swear I could spend every night of my life tangled up with her. She groans into my mouth, her chest arching into me, her fingers snaking up my back to pull my shirt off. Her eyes widen, a playful smirk curving her lips when she sees the ink covering my chest and abdomen.

"Later, I'm going to explore these in detail." She slides her fingers down my stomach, hooking onto the waistband of my jeans as she presses kisses along my collar bone.

"What are you going to do right now?" I sweep her hair to the side and hook a hand behind her neck so I can see her eyes.

She glances up, her baby blues trusting with a touch of vulnerability that I want to erase. "Enjoy this moment with you."

Fuck. *How the hell does this girl always manage to undo me?*

"Good answer, babe." I undress her slowly, savoring the sight of her body beneath mine.

She inhales sharply, her arm crossing over her chest.

"Uh-uh. No covering up for me. You're too beautiful for that." I nip at her bottom lip, freeing it from her teeth. I kiss her again, drowning in the intoxicating sensations coursing between us. Drowning in her.

My forearms balance me over Emma as I kiss her over and over again. She moans into my mouth, arching against me. My fingers trail paths up and down her body like they can't memorize her skin fast enough.

Palming her breast, I drop my head, drawing her nipple into my mouth, loving how she squirms beneath me.

Her hands make quick work of the button on my jeans and the moment her fingers slide into my boxers and find me, I see fucking stars. Emma's hands and mouth glide over my skin, caressing and kissing and making me feel so many goddamn things at once. I pay attention to her other breast, taking my time to appreciate the sounds that fall from her mouth before I drop lower.

"Don't stop." Emma commands, her hands clutching my hair.

"I got you, babe."

And I do. I work Emma over until she crests and crashes and I'm so fucking needy for her, I can't see straight.

"Baby, tell me what you want. We can pause this, go on a real date first, take things slow."

"I want you."

"You sure?"

"Please, Luke." Her fingernails dig into the tops of my shoulders.

I pull back one last time, meeting her gaze, searching her eyes for even the tiniest hesitation. But they're open and clear and wanting. She nods, granting me permission and I sigh in relief, in anticipation. Reaching into my bedside table, I grab a condom and roll it on in record time. Pressing a sensual kiss against her lips, I push inside her.

"Luke." It's a whisper, a breath on her lips.

I feel her everywhere. Her hands, her lips, her breath moving over my skin. We lose ourselves in each other. Beneath the sheets, cut off from the world, time seems to freeze.

I work her over slowly at first, building the friction between us until it's a goddamn frenzy. Lust coats her irises, sparking a fire that ignites in their blue depths.

We crash into each other and it's the sweetest serenity I've ever known.

Like a fucking homecoming.

"Oh my God," She breathes out, her hand clutching her heart as I roll next to her, tucking her into my side.

We're silent, our irregular breathing the only sounds interrupting the quiet.

"You okay, babe?"

She nods but I need to hear the words.

"You sure?" I press.

"Yeah. I just, that was," she shakes her head, "I've never experienced anything like that. It's never been like that for me before." She sounds dazed, but her eyes bore into mine with an honesty so sincere, something shifts in my chest.

I lean forward, kissing her again. "It's never been like that for me either."

She smiles shyly at my words, pure sunshine radiating from her face.

"Be with me, Em."

She shifts closer to me, looking up, her eyes heavy with sleep. "Hmm?"

"Do this with me. For real. I can't promise you fancy dates or weekend getaways. Right now, all my money is tied up in Barracuda and I work seven nights a week. I know I'm shit company most of the time and have nothing to really offer you. But babe, every spare second I have, I want to spend it with you. Get you underneath me before we pass out, wake up to your beautiful face, and steal the moments we can in between."

Emma's eyes widen as she pulls back to stare at me. "You want to date me? For real?"

"For real."

"Am I even your type?"

I frown, my eyebrows dipping low. "My type?"

"Yeah. I don't know. I picture you with a size-two blond model."

I chuckle, the sound vibrating in my chest. "Those girls are a dime a dozen, babe. I want you. I don't have a type. But I'd bet if you did, it wouldn't be me."

"What? Passionate and family-oriented? You're exactly my type, Luke."

I drop my mouth to hers, kissing her long and hard. "Then be with me."

"Yes." Such a simple word and yet, it rings with so much promise.

A promise I want to keep.

17

EMMA

The click of my heels echoes in the empty hallway as I walk to Senator LeBeau's office. These early mornings at the office, coupled with late nights at Barracuda and even later nights at Luke's, are starting to take their toll. My body aches with fatigue.

Slowing my pace, I admire my surroundings: the marble floors, the strategically placed busts, the paintings watching over me. I'm working in the U.S. Capitol Building. Well, kind of. Allowing myself to appreciate this fact fills me with gratitude, a renewed energy that reminds me I am working toward a goal and I can do this. Even with bags under my eyes.

Reinvigorated, I stop dawdling and continue to the senator's office. I am nearly at the door when the soft gait of another pair of shoes causes me to look up.

Senator Preston Harrington.

"Good morning Senator."

"Good morning. Emma, isn't it?"

"Yes, sir."

"So, you're working at the bar with Lucas and Grayson."

"Yes, sir."

He smiles, but it's a surface smile, a politician's smile, the one he's accustomed to giving at any given moment to any person deemed necessary. "Grayson tells me you're interested in pursuing a career in government. Women's health, I believe, is a cause you wish to champion?"

My heartbeats increase in tempo. *Grayson spoke to the senator about me? About the issues I care about?* This could be huge. This could be the opportunity I need to secure a job.

"Yes, sir. Women's health and family issues such as maternity and paternity leave and affordable childcare costs. I would really like to work on issues that give women and men in our country more support in family planning."

"You sound very passionate, Emma." He glances at his watch. "I've got to start my day but why don't we have lunch to discuss some of your ideas, and plans for the future. Say, Thursday, 1:00 PM?"

My heart nearly stops and explodes out of my chest at the same time. *Holy guacamole.*

I can't stop the goofy grin that spreads across my face. "That would be great. Thank you, Senator."

"Thursday then." Turning on his heel, he enters his office.

I wait until he's inside before unlocking the door to Senator LeBeau's office and pretty much hyperventilate just inside the door.

"I'M HAVING lunch with your uncle this week." I tell Luke while we wipe down bottles behind the bar.

His hands still on the neck of a bottle of Bombay Sapphire and he whips his head toward me. "You are?"

"Yeah. You sound surprised."

"Why are you having lunch with him?"

"Why?"

"Yeah. That's weird. He never asks anyone to lunch unless it's somehow in his best interest."

"He invited me to discuss my future more, you know, the issues I want to work on. It's not that weird. Loads of Senators have lunch with their interns over the course of the semester to offer some mentoring and advice."

"Uncle Preston doesn't."

"Maybe he's doing it because we're, you know. And I'm friends with Gray."

"I doubt it." He sighs, gripping the back of his neck. "Babe, be careful, okay?" Luke tucks a strand of hair behind my ear and I lean into his touch. "Preston Harrington isn't the most trustworthy guy. Any time spent with him, even an innocent lunch, always serves a motive for him."

"I'll be fine, Luke. It's just lunch."

Apprehension and frustration swirl deep in Luke's eyes and while he's confirming my suspicions that there is tension between him and Senator Harrington, all I can focus on is that he's concerned about me.

"I'll be fine."

"Let's get out of here. I hate talking about my uncle." He admits. We finish wiping down the bar and I wait for Luke to lock up.

"It almost smells like winter," I grin as he laces our fingers together and we start walking up Eighth Street.

"What does winter smell like?"

"Leaves and cold and fire. You know, hot chocolate weather."

"You cold, babe?"

"A little." I admit as Luke tugs me closer into his side.

"I didn't mean to snap about Uncle Preston. I just, I don't want you to get hurt."

"Why would I get hurt?"

Luke pauses, thinking over his words. "He's not forth-coming. Or honest."

"Most politicians aren't."

"Babe, please, just be careful, okay?"

"Worried about me?"

"Always." He admits and the confession turns my insides to mush. "That's why I come on Wednesdays to help you close; I hate the thought of you walking to the metro alone in the dark. It's different when I know Gray's with you." He shakes his head. "I still have no idea why he pawned his shifts off on you."

I wrinkle my nose, glancing up at him. "He didn't really pawn them on me; I begged for them."

"What? I thought he begged you to take them?"

"Nope, the begging was all me."

"Why, babe?" His voice thickens with concern as he slows his pace, turning me to face him. His hands settle on my hips and I have no choice but to look up and admit the one thing I've been hiding this semester.

"Things are just a bit tough right now for my parents. Financially speaking. My brother, sister, and I are all in college and my sister Celia is a junior in high school. I'm just trying to help out, start paying my own way, so my parents could focus on Celia. But I oversold it."

"What do you mean?"

"I told my dad about Barracuda and that things were going so well, I wouldn't need him to send money for rent."

"Ah."

"And then I panicked because I couldn't cover my rent."

Understanding flickers across Luke's face as he drops his head back. "So you asked Gray."

"I asked Gray, and then he made it sound like it was his idea. I think so I wouldn't be embarrassed."

"Babe, you could have told me. I could have rearranged the schedule."

"I was embarrassed."

Luke pulls me closer, wrapping me into a hug. "How are you with money now? Okay for rent?"

"Yes, I'm good."

"I'm serious."

"So am I."

"Babe, you need anything, and I mean, anything, you tell me, yeah? We're figuring stuff out between us, Em, but I care about you. I don't want you walking alone at night, I don't want you putting yourself in danger, so please, just let me know how I can help with whatever you need."

"Okay."

"Promise me."

"I promise." I say, just before Luke's mouth covers mine.

MY FINGERS GRIP the strap of my purse nervously as I walk down the steps of the Capitol Building and turn onto Eighth Street to meet Senator Harrington for lunch at The Brussels Cafe.

When I arrive at the restaurant, I'm relieved to see that Senator Harrington is already seated at a table near the back. Good. I would have felt awkward telling the hostess the reservations are for two. Under Harrington. Something about it just screams "rendezvous" even though it's a legitimate business lunch. Right?

Squaring my shoulders, I take a deep breath to calm myself and paste a smile on my face. Making my way through the tables, he notices me when I'm several steps away.

He smiles, but his eyes are cold. Ice blue. "Emma," he stands, pulling out a chair for me.

"Hi, Senator. Thanks for inviting me to meet for lunch."

He sits back down and places his napkin over his knee. "My pleasure."

Just then, the waitress pops by the side of our table, and I'm so freaking relieved that I could kiss her. *Why am I so nervous?* I never feel this way around Senator LeBeau.

"Can I get some drinks for you?" she asks pleasantly, although I don't miss the way her eyes dart between me and the senator as if assessing the relationship between us. Awkward!

"I'll take a Diet Coke, please." I pick up the menu, scanning it even though I obviously am going to order the mussels and French fries.

"Just water. Sparkling."

"Great. Do you need a few minutes with the menu, or are you all set to order?"

"I'm ready if you are." Harrington smiles, but it's directed at the pretty waitress.

"I'll have the mussels. And fries please." I hand her my menu.

"I'll have the same. So, Emma," he leans forward, clasping his hands together, "women's health issues is what you're angling for on the Hill?"

"Yes, I'm really interested in women's health and legislation aimed at creating more favorable outcomes for growing families."

"Such as?"

"Paid maternity and paternity leave. Something that's more substantial than three unpaid months. Affordable child-care options. Sick leave or paid family time off for when a child is sick," I rattle off.

Harrington considers my words.

"Thank you." He smiles at the waitress as she drops off our drinks, lemon wedges secured to the rims of the glasses.

I squeeze my lemon above my Diet Coke before dropping it in and giving a little swirl with my straw while I wait for the Senator to say something. Anything. *Why am I so freaking nervous?*

"If you had to choose one of your issues to delve into, which one would it be?" He asks after a beat, still not giving anything away.

This. This is what I need to learn. Gray was right. I am way too easy to read. I mean, here I am sitting across from Senator Harrington, telling him exactly what I'm interested in pursuing, and I still have no clue what he thinks on any of the discussed subjects. *Poker face, where are you?*

"Parental leave."

"You answered quickly."

My shoulders pinch together as nerves skate up and down my arms. *Should I have taken more time? Was he expecting something else? Aargh! What is the right way to do this?*

"I know what I'm interested in pursuing."

"Good. Why parental leave?"

I take a sip of my Diet Coke, deliberately stalling. "I think women's health issues in regards to access to abortions and various birth controls are too hot of an issue right now. They're too divisive and it will be challenging to reach a bipartisan agreement. Time will drag on; things will be stalled. The side in favor of allowing women to make their own choices regarding their bodies will continue to rally support behind it and the side opposed will continue to try to dismantle and defund organizations like Planned Parenthood as quickly as possible. And during this time, both sides will be engaged in discussions with no real action happening."

Senator Harrington sits up straighter at the edge in my voice. I mean, come on, how can a bunch of old men have the audacity to rule on women's health? Shouldn't this be a topic for women to discuss? But I digress...

"Affordable childcare is an issue that faces everyone. Both men and women. And it's not as divisive of a topic. Most people want to provide their children with more than they themselves had, and it's becoming harder and harder to do that with the cost of childcare. Nearly thirty percent of women in the US who would like to remain in the workforce are leaving after having children because childcare costs are higher than their earnings. Now the workforce is losing the skills and minds of many talented people instead of retaining them, all because they decide to have families." I shake my head. "That's really sad. It's like people are being punished for wanting to have children. It's like women are being punished for wanting to be mothers and still maintain their careers. Not to mention it's pretty embarrassing for a developed country, don't you think?"

Senator Harrington looks at me, speechless for a moment.

Ah crap. I probably shouldn't have flipped it on him in the end, but I couldn't help it. If I'm lucky enough to have a lunch with the senator, I might as well use it for some good, right? Even if I am so nervous that my sweaty palms are seeping moisture through the material of my pencil skirt.

After a beat, the senator nods. "Paid family leave and affordable childcare are bipartisan issues. I'll look into it more and see if this is something I can collaborate on with

Senator LeBeau. Email your points, with supporting research, to my Chief of Staff, Rob Del Marco."

I practically fall out of my chair.

He's taking me seriously? And talking to LeBeau?

Oh my God. I could actually end up working on something I care about. This is the best. Day. Ever.

"That would be awesome. Thank you."

Senator Harrington nods at me. "Thank you." He grins again as the waitress drops off our mussels. "So tell me, Emma, how is it working with my son?"

I bite into a French fry immediately.

Uh, what?

18

LUKE

I wake with a start, my eyes frantically swinging to the digital clock on my nightstand.

7:03 AM.

I've only overslept by three minutes, not the three hours I imagined.

Uncle P: Lucas. Need to talk. Meet me for breakfast at the cafe on K street. 8AM sharp.

I roll my eyes. Only a douchebag would feel the need to add "sharp" to a text message. Well, Uncle P does fit the bill. Standing up, I tug on a T-shirt and hoodie and lace up my sneakers.

Grabbing my wallet and keys, I plug headphones into my iPhone and close the door behind me. May as well get my daily run in and clear my head, before I have to talk to Preston Harrington about anything.

It's 8:02 AM when I walk into the cafe.

Immediately, I spot Uncle P in a booth near the back but my steps falter as I watch him exchange words with a hulking figure in a black hoodie. His eyes dart around to make sure no one is paying attention, and I slip behind a coat rack to remain unseen. The guy in the hoodie takes off, his pace brisk, his head bent low and his hood pulled up. He passes me on his way to the exit but I can't make out any of his facial features. When he pushes open the door, I note the Spade tattoo on the outside of his left hand, just below his pinkie finger.

Gang-related.

What the hell is Uncle P doing exchanging words with a guy in a local gang?

"Morning," I greet Uncle Preston, sliding into the booth across from him.

"You're late."

"What do we need to talk about?"

"Have some coffee, Lucas. You look tired."

I smile up at the waitress who stops at our table. "Coffee, black. And an egg white omelet with turkey, broccoli, and onions, please."

She nods. "Salsa on the side?"

"That'd be great." I hand her my menu.

"Toast? Home fries?"

"Dry, whole wheat, please. No home fries."

"You got it." She turns toward Uncle P.

"Just a coffee with cream."

"Nothing to eat?"

He cuts me a look and I smile patiently.

"An English muffin with two scrambled eggs."

She nods again and disappears with our menus.

"I thought we'd have coffee, not a damn event."

"It's just breakfast, Uncle P. Now, what do we need to talk about?"

"You didn't heed my advice. You're fighting Joe Carney in December."

I nod.

"You sure about that? It's going to be a tough fight." He continues.

I shrug.

Our waitress drops off our drinks.

"I'd hate to see you blow everything you have going on with the restaurant to get your ass kicked in the ring." He takes a sip of his coffee and then adds more cream. His movements are methodical and measured. As if we're sitting here to have an actual uncle-nephew catchup about our lives instead of him demanding that I meet him for a reason I've yet to figure out. "I need that money back by January, Lucas."

"If I win, I can pay you back in full."

"But the odds are you won't win." He smiles his thanks to the waitress as she sets down our food. Piling some eggs on his English muffin, he takes a bite, chewing thoughtfully. "You do know that, right? You're not going to win, Lucas. You're just going to end up hurt with a pile of medical bills to pay on top of the money you owe me."

"I'll take that chance, Uncle P. How're your eggs?"

He puts his cutlery down and leans forward, his voice menacingly quiet. "You think this is a big joke? I've got a lot on the line, Lucas, too much for someone like you to even comprehend. You will not win this fight. Drop out now while you can still do so gracefully."

"We've already had this conversation. I don't see what my taking a fight has to do with you having 'a lot on the line'."

"I wouldn't expect you to."

I let that comment roll off my shoulders and take a bite of my omelet. "I've already made it clear that I'm not dropping the fight. Is there anything else you want to discuss?"

"Always so stubborn. Just like your father. Don't you think you should have learned from his recklessness?"

I see fucking red.

Dropping my fork and knife and gripping the edge of the table until my knuckles turn white, I remind myself to shut it down. Rein in the anger. Uncle P is baiting me for a reaction, and if I give it to him, give him what he wants, he wins. I take a few deep breaths, dropping my head to study my omelet and toast while I calm down. "Is there anything else that needs to be discussed?"

"No."

I nod, shoving a few more forkfuls of food in my mouth. "Then I better get back to my run. Thanks for breakfast."

***

THE POUND of the vinyl against my fist feels good, smooth, natural as I work around the heavy bag. Bobbing and weaving, I clear my mind from everything except boxing. My hands ache but I keep going, focusing on the next jab, the next cross. I imagine my opponent, the blood thirst in his eyes, the way he comes at me. But I don't give an inch. I'm fighting for my future.

When Scoop agreed to take me on, he said he would push me to my limits. He is. Now that I'm doing this legit, no more shady garage fights, no more beating some has-been in a back alley, or going toe-to-toe in an abandoned firehouse, I'm committed to seeing it through. I'm going to make something of myself, for myself. Sure, I'm technically a business owner. But does it count if you didn't build the business? Does it count when the whole thing is just handed over to you because of someone else's loss, grief, desperation?

I don't know.

But this, boxing, this is all mine.

Despite, or maybe because of Uncle P's digs, his attempt

to plant seeds of doubt in my mind that I'm going to lose, I'm fully committed to doing this. In fact, his trying to convince me to drop the fight has only served to motivate me. To push me past my mental limitations. To make me realize that I was making excuses for myself, and these excuses were holding me back. Now, I'm all in.

I'm going to be someone Emma can be proud of.

The bag swings back and I jab with my left, slipping quickly to the side to avoid the trajectory of the bag as it swings back again. *Jab, jab, cross.*

"You're getting better. Faster." Scoop comments from the side of the ring, where Ammo is giving Ramos some pointers.

"You need to focus more on your footwork." He nods toward my sneakers. "Today, Ammo is stepping into the ring with you. He's going to go all out, so you better bring it if you don't want to be eating the canvas." He tosses me a water bottle and a mouth guard.

I catch both, gulping down some of the water and popping the guard into my mouth. Fucking A. Ammo is a beast. He's been on the circuit for over five years and while most people think he's faded, that he should have retired by now, he still fights. Sure, he's stepped back more over the past year to focus on coaching, but I know better than to underestimate him.

"What's up, man?" Ammo asks, as I climb into the ring and Ramos drops out. "You ready for this?"

I nod even though there's no way anyone could ever be ready to face off against Ammo. He's in a heavier weight class than me, so going up against him will be brutal.

"I've been watching you the last few days." He drags a palm across his face and I wait, hanging on his every word, for any morsel of knowledge he's about to drop. "You favor your right side too much. You got to get more confident with your left jab. Make your combinations crisper. You're too sloppy. And your feet," he shakes his head, "I know Scoop's running you through drills for speed, but you need to pick it up, yeah?"

"Alright."

"Okay then. Let's do this."

"Tap gloves. Start on the bell," Scoop says from the side, nodding at Ramos, a fifteen-year-old kid who loves to hang around the gym, doing whatever needs doing, posing as Scoop's shadow. Kid's got a tough home life and the guys at the gym are his second family. Everyone likes him, and he idolizes the guys, especially Scoop and Ammo.

Ammo and I tap gloves and the bell sounds. He cuts me clean across the left side of my jaw before I even take a breath.

"Get your gloves up," Scoop yells.

Raising my hands to better protect my face, Ammo and I circle each other, pawing. Once, twice, three times. I throw a jab and it glances off his forearm. Blocked. He tsks at me. My temper flares as he tosses me a cavalier smile.

I toss out a wild punch that lands awkwardly on his shoulder.

"Focus, man. Don't let your temper rule you. Rule your temper."

I bite my lip, taking a second to steady my emotions.

Ammo comes at me again, but I block this punch.

"That's it. Move your feet." Scoop calls out. "Luke, stop pulling your punches and commit."

We go on like this, around and around, for four rounds of three minutes each. I'm sweating buckets, the back of my shirt sticking to me like a second skin, my eyes stinging with the drops of sweat that fall into them. Ammo works up a decent sweat but doesn't look anything like me.

I'm beyond relieved when Ramos finally rings the bell, signaling the end of our exchange.

Ammo nods at me. "You did good. Most guys can't last this long with me."

"Thanks, man. Appreciate that, because I'm winded as fuck."

"You're out of shape," Scoop comments on the obvious.

"Guess so." I take a swig from the bottle of water Ramos passes me.

"We'll fix it. But we don't have a lot of time." Scoop passes me a sheet of paper. "This is your new workout. This is your new meal plan." He moves his hand underneath the sheet of paper and flips it for me. "You need to cut down on some of your weight. Stop eating that fried food from your restaurant. And get faster, leaner."

"Meaner," Ammo throws out. "Work on your feet, protect your left side, keep your head up. Make your combinations sharper, crisper. You're a fringe contender so people aren't expecting you to blow this out of the water, but that doesn't mean you can't."

I nod to everything they're saying, even though I'm not sure my brain is absorbing any of it. All I can think about is getting more air into my lungs before I collapse.

"Show up every day committed, dedicated, ready to train," Scoop advises. "Follow this meal plan, prep your meals, lift in the evenings or early mornings. I don't give a fuck when you do it as long as you do it. You follow this." He points to the paper again, "and you may even be ready in time to fight Lightning."

My head snaps up at this. "You really think I have a shot?" I'm still so winded from sparring with Ammo that I'm beginning to think Lightning will knock me out in the first round.

"That depends on you."

He's right. All of this depends on me. But I've never been one to back down from a challenge, and hell if I'll start now.

"If you're hungry enough, he could be yours, kid," Ammo throws out.

"I'm hungry."

"Be starving." Scoop's voice is gruff, serious as he fixes me with a look. "I'll see you Monday. We're kicking it up a few notches now. Show up ready to train, committed, dedicated. I demand nothing but focus. No dicking around. You wanna act like a bitch, you've got no right being in my ring."

"I'll do everything you tell me," I swear.

"I hear that a lot. I'll wait and see if you mean it. Now get out of here."

"You did good, man." Ramos pats me on the back. "The last guy that got in the ring with Ammo didn't last two minutes."

"Thanks, Ramos."

"See you Monday." He lopes off after Scoop and Ammo.

I climb out of the ring, sauntering off toward the showers. My body aches from the punches Ammo landed. I need to toughen up. Not just physically, but mentally. Emotionally. I need to do this. To prove to myself that I can.

To prove to Emma that I'm worth it.

Worth something.

NOVEMBER

19

EMMA

Under the Family and Medical Leave Act (1993 – really? It's so recent.), employers are required to allow an employee up to twelve weeks of *unpaid* leave following the birth or adoption of a child. During this time, your employer must still provide your benefits and can't give your job away to someone else.

Gee, how big of them.

I want to bang my head on the table.

Especially after noting that parents in Sweden can take up to 480 days off at 80% of their pay *after* new mamma bears take the eighteen weeks due to them for maternity leave. How in Iceland, parents split the nine-months post-childbirth leave in half - three months for mom, three months for dad, and three to be decided however it works best for the family. Even Estonia gives mothers 140 days of 100% paid pregnancy and maternity leave with dads getting two weeks of paid time off to bond with their little one. Come on! Nothing against Estonia, but we all know that the Scandinavian countries are light-years ahead of us with social and family policies. But Estonia? They just left the Soviet Union in 1991.

And they already managed to surpass the United States in their commitment to families.

These statistics are insane. For a developed country, this is really embarrassing not to mention inefficient, ineffective, and a giant waste of talent.

Reaching up to tug on my bangs, I yank a little too hard in frustration.

"Easy there, or you'll end up bald," Gray scolds me, placing a Diet Coke by my folder of articles.

"This is so annoying," I say instead, taking a sip of the sticky sweet Cola.

"What's annoying, Stanton?" He braces his arms against the bar, his biceps bulging under his tight T-shirt.

"Do you do that on purpose?"

"Do what?"

"Stand in ways that showcase your muscles? You're like a woman intentionally trying to flaunt her cleavage."

"She's got you there," Luke chuckles behind me. "Hey," he says softly, raking his fingers through my hair before wrapping his hand around the back of my neck and squeezing as he dips his head and brushes a kiss to the corner of my mouth.

"Hi," I whisper back, drinking him in. He's sporting some scruff, his hair a little too long on top, untamed, just the way I like it. Ripped jeans hang low on his hips and his tattoos glow against his white T-shirt. He grins at me and something lightens in his eyes. Something I want to keep there and hold on to.

"You guys are disgusting." Gray's voice booms and I swivel back on my barstool.

"You never answered my question, Gray."

"No, Stanton, I don't deliberately try to show off my incredible physique. You can stop with your judgey looks now. I don't think it's fair to penalize me for being naturally athletic, hot as fuck, and having a body girls can't tear their eyes away from." He says it seriously, but amusement flickers in the dark brown of his eyes.

"Don't forget modest and humble," I add.

Luke chuckles again.

"There's also that," Gray agrees.

"What are you reading?" Luke peers over my shoulder at the article lying on top of the bar.

"Something that annoys her," Gray throws out.

"It is annoying," I say. "Look at this," I point to the headline. "'USA one of only four Countries Without Paid Parental Leave.' It's a disgrace that the value of creating families in our country has been diminished to this. It's like people don't want women to reenter the workforce after giving birth. It makes me so angry to think that one day, if I'm lucky enough to be a mom, I'll have a baby and, if I work for the US government, I'll have to seriously decide if I can continue my career and put my baby in daycare that costs more than I earn or if I should stay home for a few years until my baby is old enough to go to school but by then I'll have been out of the rat race for too long to have the desired skill set. And, I'll have to wonder about all of this while I return to work after like five seconds off because who can survive with no money? Better pray I don't need a C-section so I can at least walk standing upright, hope postpartum doesn't get me down and I just have the normal waves of emotional and hormonal ups and downs while I leave my newborn baby with a stranger so we can keep the lights on."

Gray and Luke stare at me in a mixture of horror and confusion.

"Are you guys having a baby?" Gray asks, his eyebrows disappearing into his hairline.

"No!" I smack the article with my palm. "This is serious, though. Your dad is even co-sponsoring the legislation to pass a bill for fairer parental leave."

His expression changes from humorous, to thoughtful, to confused, to suspicious. "Why?"

"Why?" I repeat. Once again, parrot Emma at your service. "Because this is a really important issue facing millions of people in our country."

Gray shakes his head. Behind me, Luke stiffens and the pressure on the back of my neck increases. "It's not an issue he cares about," Gray says dismissively. "It doesn't make any sense that he would propose something like this."

My chest constricts at his words, my stomach sinking. Gray just confirmed that his dad doesn't care about this issue. It's not in his policy repertoire. Yet after we had lunch and I expressed an interest, he called Senator LeBeau, and proposed co-sponsoring this bill. Then, he requested that I be part of the research team.

I should be elated and part of me is.

Still, something fishy is going on. And deep down, I know it has to do with me, Luke, and Gray. Or the relationship between us. Somehow, we're involved in Harrington's machinations, whether we know it or not.

I look down at the article again, a coldness skating up my spine. "I don't know."

Gray shakes his head, turning around to grab a rag and wipe up the bar. "You should pack up. The dinner rush will be starting soon," he tells me, his chin jutting toward my folder.

I nod, shuffling my articles into the folder and shoving it into my bag.

Luke squeezes the back of my neck one more time before letting his hand drop and grabbing the straps of my bag. He passes it over the bar to Gray, who stashes it in the spot I use to hold all my crap.

But his eyes stay trained on me, narrowing slightly, his jaw clenched. "Be careful, Em." He breathes out.

When I meet his gaze, concern and a flash of anger lurk dangerously.

Whatever Harrington is up to, it's not good.

———

MY SHIFT DRAGS ON FOREVER.

Once Barracuda closes, Gray heads home, and Luke and I head back to his place. Or, more accurately, to his bed.

As Luke undresses me, his gaze drinking me in, his hands tracing the lines of my body, my worry from earlier magically melts away. Instead, I lose myself in Luke.

Slow, languid movements, hot kisses, breathless words, and a joining so sweet that emotion wells in my throat and behind my eyes. He's reverent. He looks at me like I'm his next breath, touches me like I may disappear, and holds me like he never wants to let me go.

I hope he doesn't.

Hours later, my hair splayed across Luke's pillow, the line of his body pressing against me, his tattooed fingers resting lightly on my stomach, his chest against my back, I feel every sensation and want to memorize it. Luke snores in my ear and I grin to myself. As exhausted as I am, I can't sleep. I can't turn off my heart from grasping at every moment I get to spend in Luke's embrace.

And I can't turn my head off from racing with various scenarios to explain why Harrington would propose the legislation, why Gray would be confused, why Luke would be concerned. And most of all, what is connecting the three of us to motivate Harrington to make a move?

What does he want?

And what the hell does it have to do with me?

"You're burning out." Gray's voice cuts through the fog in my head.

I hear him, and yet his voice sounds muffled. As if he's talking to me underwater. I pull my eyes up to his and the movement causes fireworks to explode in my head.

My head is pounding, and I can hear my pulse in my eardrums. Dropping my highlighter, I blink at him across the bar with what I imagine are bleary, red eyes. "Huh?"

He hunches forward, staring into my eyes.

"If you wanted to have a staring contest, you could have just – ah, you blinked. I win." I attempt to divert his attention from studying me, but the opposite occurs. Concern flickers in Gray's eyes as I raise my hand victoriously before dropping it limply back to my manila folder of articles. Damn, this research project is going to end me.

"Stanton, you're exhausted."

"I'm fine, just tired." I pull my sweater tighter around my shoulders. "Why the hell is it freezing in here? Is the heat working?" I can't be exhausted. Team no sleep right here! I have to make at least $130 tonight to cover my rent without dipping into my savings account. Rent that is due in three days.

Adulting is so, so hard.

I am so, so tired.

I blink slowly.

Did I just doze off thinking about my rent?

"Stanton." Gray's fingers close around my wrist. "Go home."

"I'm fine, really. Can you pass me a Red Bull?"

"Hey, babe. You okay?" Luke walks up behind me, dropping a quick kiss to the top of my head.

"No," Gray shakes his head, answering for me. "She's so tired, she's about to fall right off the barstool and take a nap on this disgusting floor."

Ah, a nap. Even on this floor, I would do it. If just given fifteen uninterrupted minutes.

Luke's fingers curl under my chin as he turns my head to look at him. Whatever he sees must be concerning beyond my usual disheveldness (is that even a word?), because his jaw tightens and his eyes grow wary. "Emma?"

I blink again, allowing his beautiful face to come back into focus. "Hi."

Luke holds the back of his hand up to my forehead. "Fuck. Baby, you're burning up."

I snort unattractively, my eyes cutting to Gray. "You shouldn't say such things in front of other people." I try to swat Luke but lose my balance, teetering on the edge of the barstool.

I wait for Gray's laugh but am met with silence. Silence and the stormy eyes of two broody men staring at me like I've lost the plot. Maybe I have.

"Em," Luke's voice is gentle. A word I would never use to describe him. Ever. "I'm going to take you home so you can rest, okay? You need to sleep. You're sick, baby." His fingers close around my elbow as he guides me off the barstool.

I slide off and wince as my feet hit the ground, the impact jarring up my spine and into my throbbing head. Oh jeez, Louise. I am sick.

"I can't be sick." I say, my voice so deep I sound more like a man than Luke. Sad day. "I need to make $130 to cover my rent and it's due in three days. Three days!"

Luke's eyes blaze with frustration as he swears softly. Behind me, Gray clucks at me. Like a mother freaking hen.

"Guys, this is serious."

Luke swings me up into his arms so quickly I don't even grasp the movement until I'm settled against his chest and my perspective of the ceiling is different. He needs to paint.

"Gray, I'm taking her to my place. I'll be back to help you out. If you get swamped, see if Hector can pop out of the kitchen for a bit to bus tables and run food."

"No problem, dude." Gray answers in that casual, unaffected way of his. I wonder if he's ever been stressed out in his life. So stressed and overwhelmed that he, say, gives himself the bubonic plague.

Because that's how I'm starting to feel. Now that I'm nestled against Luke's soft sweater and hard muscular chest, I allow myself to relax for the first time in what feels like a lifetime.

My throat is sore, my bones are cold, and I feel like a jackhammer is on a repeating loop in my brain.

It's official. I'm dying.

But if I have to go, at least I can drift off with the clean soap, pine cones, all-Luke, spicy man scent washing over me.

Silver. Lining.

———

THE SOFT PILLOW under my cheek is a welcome greeting back into the world of the living. I wake slowly, unsure how many hours have passed. The comforting scent of Luke is still wrapped around me like a hug, which could be explained since I'm at his apartment, laying in his bed, wearing one of his T-shirts.

Happy sigh.

I snuggle deeper under his thick duvet, rolling over onto his side of the bed. It's empty. Huh? I slam my palm down on the nightstand, feeling blindly for my phone, until my fingers connect with the charger. Snaking my hand up the cord, I grasp my phone and pull it toward me, checking the time.

11:23 PM.

Oh my God! I've missed work! But how could I have missed work when I'm in the boss's bed? That just sounds bad. Wait a second…

Bolting upright, I flip on the bedside lamp. Next to the phone charger is a bottle of water with a scrap of paper tucked underneath.

Em,

If you wake up before I get home, help yourself to some takeout in the fridge. Advil is next to the stove. If your fever spikes, take some. There's tea and hot chocolate and those cookies you like on the counter. Sweet dreams.

Luke

I smile at his messy, slanted handwriting.

Reminders of my foggy head and aching joints come back to me slowly as I recall this afternoon at Barracuda. Gray and Luke ordering me home to rest. Luke carrying me into his room, changing my clothes, and tucking me into bed like a child. It felt so good, so nostalgic, to be cared for like that.

Stretching my arms overhead, I force myself to wake up. I swing my legs over the side of the bed and stand slowly, still feeling out of sorts. Dizzy. Fuzzy. Flu-like.

I make my way into the kitchen and sure enough, a box of rainbow chocolate chip cookies from Stella's sits on the counter. I snag one while I make myself a mug of hot chocolate. Revived by the sugar, I pass on the Thai takeout and collapse on the couch, picking up the remote control to flip through the channels.

Luke's iPad is open on the coffee table, a running log of various boxing matches and other sports updates constantly lighting up the screen. And then, I swear I wasn't purposely snooping, a text message. From Uncle Preston.

Senator Preston Harrington, you continue to confuse the hell out of me!

Uncle Preston: Lucas, I need to speak with you. Are you home? I'm stopping by in ten.

Oh my God! What do I do? What do I do?

I scramble back into Luke's bedroom to grab my phone off the end table and frantically call Luke for advice.

One ring. Two rings. Three rings. Voicemail.

Hanging up, I toss the phone back on the bed and run around like a crazy person searching for my clothes. I finally find them neatly folded next to the bathroom sink. Stripping off Luke's shirt, I pull on my black jeans and work shirt.

Catching a glimpse of myself in the mirror, a crazy, hot mess, I realize that the dumbest thing I could do is answer the door. I should turn off the TV and all the lights and pretend that no one is here.

Duh. Much better plan.

Letting out a sigh of relief, I walk back into the kitchen to do just that when a knock sounds on the door.

Seriously?

I freeze.

Do I answer it? Do I let him knock? Can he hear the TV? Can he tell the lights are on? Is my fever spiking?

I'm too scared to breathe.

Two long minutes pass as I stare at the door convinced Preston Harrington can see me through it like X-Ray vision or whatever it is that superheroes, in this case the villain, possess.

After another minute passes, I slowly let out my breath and sit back on the couch. Picking up my hot chocolate, I pretend the whole thing never happened.

After all, I excel at denial.

20

LUKE

It's late when I slide into bed next to Emma, the heat of her body warming the sheets. Even my side of the bed. I place a hand over her forehead and wince that she's still running a fever. Poor Em. I've never known a girl who works as hard as she does and it's tough to see her struggle like this.

For $130 for rent.

Why didn't she just ask me for the money?

I'd pay her entire rent if it would allow her to relax a little, go out with her friends on the weekends, have some fun.

Tugging her body into mine, she automatically curls into a tiny ball, allowing me to wrap my arms around her and hold her to my chest. A little sigh escapes her parted lips and I grin, kissing the top of her head.

After several minutes, Emma's phone buzzes with an incoming FaceTime call.

Two minutes later her screen lights up again.

And again.

The fourth time, I get up and while I would never snoop

around to check her messages or anything, I peer at the screen, worried something is wrong.

Maura. One of her best friends from college.

Debating if I should wake her or not, I rub the ends of her hair between my fingers. Her eyes flutter open and she turns to look at me.

"Hey baby."

Her hand reaches out, her fingertips grazing my chin. "You're here."

"You doing okay, babe?"

She stares at me for several seconds as the sleepiness clouding her eyes recedes. "Your uncle came by."

I scrunch my eyebrows in confusion, but my blood turns cold. *Uncle Preston? Why?* "What did he want?"

"I don't know. I was scared to open the door."

"Why, Em? You could have just told him I was at the restaurant and you were hanging out."

"I feel horrible. I just," she swallows thickly, and I can tell it pains her, "I didn't know what to say. He sent you a text and it came up on your iPad, but he knocked before I was even dressed."

I watch her for a moment, letting her words sink in. Everything she says makes sense, but I can tell there's more to it than that. *Why would she be scared?*

Dropping it since I know she's hurting, I lean over and kiss her forehead. "Don't worry about Uncle P. I'll call him in the morning. My phone died before I saw his message. Right now, we need to focus on getting you better. Did you take the Advil I left out?"

Her eyes widen at this. "I forgot. I was so flustered and –" she shakes her head, "can I have some now?"

Why the hell was she flustered?

"Of course. I'll be right back." I smooth her hair away from her face. "Oh, your friend Maura keeps calling."

"I'll talk to her tomorrow. Thanks."

I leave her in bed to grab some Advil and water from the kitchen.

Why the hell is Uncle P intimidating Emma? What the hell is going on?

"Lucas."

"Hey Uncle P. Sorry I missed you last night. I was at the restaurant until late and didn't see your text until this morning. What's up?"

"Lucas. No need to lie about it. I know you were home last night. You could have just messaged me back and told me you weren't up for a visit but to allow me to trek all the way to your place and not answer the door is rude."

"Sorry about that, Uncle P." I grind my teeth together to keep myself from saying what's on my mind... and it's a lot more colorful than an apology. But Uncle P hasn't called to collect on his loan yet and I want to keep it that way. "I was at the restaurant until late. But my girlfriend was at my place. She has the flu and —"

"Girlfriend?"

"Yeah. She's sick this week so —"

"Lucas. When were you going to bring her around? I'd love to meet her."

I pinch the bridge of my nose. That statement can't be further from the truth. *Besides, doesn't Uncle P know we're dating?*

"She's really busy, Uncle P. Works two jobs, has a lot of commitments."

"Admirable. Who is she?"

"Her name is Emma. Emma Stanton. I think you know her."

"The intern?" The bite in his voice is hard to miss, but he doesn't sound at all surprised. And this is when my suspicions are confirmed. Something is going on between Uncle P and Emma. Or better yet, Uncle P is up to something where Emma is concerned.

"Yeah. She's interning for LeBeau this semester."

Uncle P clucks his tongue, sounding bored. "I suppose it's nice to have a fling every now and then with a college girl."

I force myself to pause, to prevent the stream of nasty words I want to spew at him from spilling out. "It's not a fling. We're together and things are great. Thanks for asking."

"I hope your new girlfriend doesn't distract you from your other commitments."

"No worries there."

"It would be horrible to get caught up in the moment and not be properly prepared for your fight. Or let things at the business go and be unable to pay back your loan in January. Don't you agree?"

"Yes." I bite out.

"I hope you know what you're doing, Lucas. I need to take this call. Take care." He clicks off.

I stare at my phone and realize too late that he never said why he stopped by last night or what he needed to discuss with me.

In fact, I gave away more information than I acquired.

And that's never a good thing where Uncle Preston is concerned.

21

EMMA

The steel in his gaze stops me dead in my tracks, the clicking of my heels against the marble floor faltering before coming to a complete halt.

"Emma," he says gravely, his eyes flashing ice blue. Like the arctic.

"Hello, Senator Harrington." I smile brightly, focusing on sunshine and rainbows.

He nods at a colleague who passes in the hallway as he walks toward me, stopping when he is only inches away. "I hear you're dating my nephew."

What is it with men in positions of power who just throw it all out there, toppling you over with one freaking sentence?

No build up, no warning. Just... this.

"Yes, Luke and I are seeing each other."

Why does he care who Luke dates?

Despite seeming to have a complicated relationship with Luke, I can't imagine his being that interested in his love life. And this chat does not seem like it's going to end in a big hug and a "welcome to the family" invitation to Thanksgiving.

Harrington's eyes narrow and he stands taller, towering over me.

Is this an intimidation tactic?

Does it matter? It's working.

I suddenly feel very nervous, very small, and very silly standing here in my pencil skirt and nude heels, tugging on my bangs and desperately wishing I had my purse so my fingers could clasp onto the strap of the bag instead of flailing around with nothing to settle on.

"Why?"

My mouth gapes open. "Why?"

"Surely someone of your caliber, an intelligent, well-educated, passionate young woman isn't really interested in dating someone like Luke."

I think my jaw drops farther, if that's possible. It's not lost on me that he didn't add "pretty" to that list of compliments. Although, if he had, I would have thought it creepy. But now I'm annoyed that he didn't. I know I'm not a supermodel, but I'm not exactly lacking either. And what's that bit about me not interested in dating someone like Luke? *What does that even mean?*

"I'm not sure what you mean," I bite out, congratulating myself for keeping my voice even.

"Oh, come on, Emma. You're a smart girl."

"You said that already."

"What's your ulterior motive?"

"Motive?"

He nods.

"I don't have one. I really, genuinely like Luke." I tell him the truth, hoping he will back off.

He laughs, which is confusing until I realize that two other bodies have entered the hallway and are about to pass us. Wow, he's good. Nothing like putting on a show for the spectators.

As soon as they pass, his laugh withers, his expression grave. "If you think dating my nephew will give you some pull here in terms of securing a job, I can assure you that it won't. Unless, of course, you are open to an additional understanding."

My eyes nearly pop out of my head. *Is he insane?* "That thought never crossed my mind." I can't help the anger that colors my tone and yet, my furious reaction seems to please Harrington as a smile flits across his lips. "And I'm not interested in any type of understanding between you and me."

"That's too bad. I was really hoping, if you care about my nephew as you say you do, that you wouldn't want him to end up hurt and humiliated."

"What are you talking about?"

"Luke's fight is next month. Convince him to drop it and I'll see what I can do about convincing LeBeau to offer you a permanent position come next year."

"No."

"That's too bad. Although I suppose it doesn't matter. Things will play out with the fight the way they're meant too." He shrugs as I glare at him. "And things with you and Luke will go nowhere. It's a dead end."

"What are you talking about?"

He leans forward, invading my space, "If you don't end your dalliance with my nephew, I'll kill the Parental Leave legislation. Bury it under so many other pressing issues that are important to the American people that you won't see the change you deem imperative for the next twenty years. Or more. Then you can tell me what purpose your presence here has actually served." He fixes me with his steely glare before walking toward his office, his pace quick and clipped.

"Wait."

He turns around, a smile playing over the corners of his lips.

"What about Luke? Were you serious about him getting hurt?"

Harrington angles his head, a splash of emotion deepening the blue of his eyes for just a second until the Ice King is back. "Yes."

I take a step toward him, about to sell my soul if he will just offer me a reassurance that Luke will be safe.

Safe from what?

He's bribing you, Emma!

But who cares if it means Luke is okay?

Harrington holds up his hand and my steps falter. "When you do end things with Luke, I'll make sure he doesn't get hurt in the fight next month. Take it as a sign of good faith between us." He grins. "I'm impressed, Emma. Didn't peg you as someone with so much... fortitude. You're getting a lot out of our understanding, aren't you? Protecting Luke and the Parental Leave legislation? Such a do-gooder." He cuts on his heel and disappears into his office.

I release the breath I was holding and stretch out an arm, searching for the wall. When my hand finally makes contact, I drop my weight against it as a flurry of emotions – anger, sadness, confusion, fear – sweep through me.

I've been bribed.

And I fell for every single thing Harrington said.

Standing here, reeling in a storm of emotions that have my knees shaking, I have no clue if he was even telling the truth.

My palms tingle with nervous energy and sweat.

What if Harrington was making the whole thing up?

What if he doesn't even know anything about Luke's fight?

But then again, what if he does?

———

"TABLE EIGHT, PEQUEÑA." Jorge thrusts the food-laden tray toward me and I stumble forward, knocking into the tray and spilling a side of rice.

"Fuck." The word leaves my mouth on a puff of air through my two front teeth.

Jorge's eyes snap up and Hector turns to look at me over his shoulder.

"You okay, Chica?" Hector asks, walking around the metal divider to replace the side of rice.

I nod, pinching the bridge of my nose. The backs of my eyes burn with a sudden surge of tears. I'm overwhelmed. I rarely curse out loud.

Hector's hand rests on my shoulder. "You're okay, Emma. Don't worry, table eight is ready to go and you're fine." His voice is low and reassuring and in this moment, I want to turn and hug him.

Instead, I pull myself together, smile through my sniffles, and heave the tray up, resting the rim on my shoulder and balancing the weight on my palm.

I'm okay. I got this. "Thanks guys." I exit the kitchen, bee lining toward table eight.

In my peripheral vision, I sense Gray behind the bar, trying to catch my eye. My shoulders stiffen under his unrelenting gaze. He knows I'm avoiding him.

Smiling widely at the customers seated at table eight, I place down their entrees and sides, explaining each dish and asking if they need refills. The entire time my lips move, my mind races.

Luke enters in the restaurant and I'm tempted to hold the tray up as a shield.

Maybe he won't notice me?

His eyes cut to me directly and I flush even though I'm not making eye contact.

I thank the table and wish them a good meal before turning away. Stacking the tray in the kitchen, I disappear into the inventory closet to take a minute.

"Why are you avoiding me?"

The door to the closet opens and closes. Luke flips on the light.

Poop. I wasn't quick enough. He found me. Deep down I knew he would.

I turn, trying to keep my eyes hidden behind my bangs. Finally, they come in handy for something.

"Hi." My fingers are twisted together and I feel warm. Too warm. And awkward.

Luke steps closer, his hands coming up on either side of the shelving unit I'm standing in front of, caging me in.

"Emma."

I blink furiously, trying to keep my tears at bay.

What am I supposed to do? To say? I can't talk to you because your uncle is intimidating me? Because I'm trying to keep you safe? Because Harrington is going to cut a piece of legislation that can provide support to millions of people if I continue to date you?

I take a deep breath to steady my nerves. *You were just a fling, Emma.* I try desperately to convince myself of this fact so I can meet his gaze and not cry. I was a semester fling. Nothing more. But even as a twinge of doubt twists in my gut, my heart knows it isn't true.

"Look at me," he commands, his voice low and gruff and... hurt.

I meet his gaze and my breath stills in my chest.

His eyes are as dark as a forest in a rainstorm, and just as stormy. Angry. Confused and vulnerable. Frustrated and… knowing.

"What's going on?"

I shake my head, the first traitor tear escaping over my lower eyelashes and tracking a trail down my cheek. If this was a movie, I would have nailed this scene. My one glistening tear was so perfectly executed.

Unfortunately, an ugly torrent of tears follows.

Within moments, I am reduced to a blabbering mess, sobbing, literally sobbing, on Luke's shoulder, my fingers twisted in his shirt.

"Baby, talk to me," he pleads, his hand cupping the back of my head, his fingers tangling in my messy ponytail.

I can't! I scream it over and over in my head but nothing comes out except a rush of tears and sounds so achingly sad, I block them out.

I block everything out.

I allow myself one more minute of crying in Luke's arms. Of being wrapped up in his warmth. Of feeling connected to him in ways my body and heart crave.

Then I disentangle myself and walk out of the closet. I tear off my apron and leave it in a heap on a discarded tray in the kitchen. I walk right out the back door, past the surprised and curious glances of Hector and Jorge, passed Luke's Blazer, away from the restaurant.

I ignore Luke's calls, pretend I don't hear the pounding of his footsteps behind me for several beats until they quiet. I walk and walk and walk.

I don't register the passing cars as I turn out of the alley onto Eighth Street. I barely feel the cold wind as it hits me squarely in the face. I don't process the rush of bodies that step around me.

I walk and walk and walk.

And eventually, I collapse in my bed, huddled under my duvet and Cassie's watchful eye, her lips tight with worry.

I cry myself into oblivion.

Cassie lets him in.

I knew she would.

She's not heartless. Not like me at all.

He paces before me like a caged animal. He can't sit still, can't stop moving. His eyes are dark and menacing. The worry from earlier, in the inventory closet, has been replaced with anger and bitterness and something deeper... something I can't place.

"I can't help you if you don't tell me what's wrong," he accuses.

"Nothing's wrong." My voice is devoid of all emotion. Monotonous. Dead.

"Em, you're not making any sense. None of this makes sense. Just a few days ago, everything between us was great. You were sleeping in my bed, I was taking care of you while you were sick, we were together. And now, this," he holds his arm out to me as if he doesn't know what to say, "I don't even know what this is. What's wrong? Something happened, and I need you to tell me what it is so I can fix it."

What is it about guys thinking they can always fix things?
Don't they know that sometimes, problems can't be fixed?
That they just are.
This is one of those times.

My heart feels heavy and I hurt. I hurt so deeply in all

facets of my body that I turn it all off so I don't feel anything except numb.

I can't be with Luke.

Being with Luke means he will get hurt in December's fight, possibly even ending his career before it has the chance to take off. Being with Luke means millions of people, mothers, fathers, adoptive parents, single parents who will end up benefitting from the Parental Leave bill will miss out. They'll all be stuck making difficult decisions about employment and childcare when they should be focused on enjoying their little ones. I can't do that. I need to keep Luke safe, to help him pursue his dream even if he can't see it that way.

Besides, maybe Harrington was right. Maybe all we ever were going to be was a dead end.

I mean, look at Luke. Standing before me, pissed at the world. His eyes flashing, his hands gesturing, his mouth moving. He still looks like Adonis. He still manages to level me with just one glance, one word, one anything. I could never be in his world long-term. He's too big, too passionate, too much. And I'm... not his type.

"Emma!" The sharpness of his voice pulls me from my thoughts.

I continue to stare at him.

He crouches down next to my bed, his line of vision even with mine. "Please, baby. Just talk to me. Please." The begging in his voice pulls at the cloud of darkness I've shrouded myself in. He reaches up to cup my cheek and I turn into his touch before I can stop myself. "Em?"

But I can't give in. I know I can't.

Taking a deep breath, I steel my will, harden my heart, and think of doing the greater good for the greatest number of people. Blah. Blah. Blah.

"It's my uncle, isn't it?"

I know my eyes widen. I know this because Luke's widen in return. His hand drops from my cheek. "What the fuck did he say to you?"

I shake my head. I know now that whatever I say, he won't believe. He knows that Harrington is behind this and whatever I say won't matter.

Still, I try.

"Luke. I can't do this anymore."

He snorts, a chortle of laughter. His hand wipes over his lower face and his eyes bore into mine.

"We can't be together." I say this so unconvincingly that it's hard to believe myself. "We were never going to work out. We come from two different worlds." *And I'd never measure up in yours.*

This seems to get his attention because he narrows his eyes, his irises glinting in anger.

"I don't want to try at this. I want to finish this semester and go back to Philadelphia. Unattached." My heart breaks at his devastated expression. *Please don't believe anything I'm saying.* "Consider this my two weeks' notice for the restaurant. I'll be out of your life in no time."

His mouth twists, anger curling his lips. "Emma." He moves closer, his stomach hitting the side of my bed. "Keep the job. I'll hire someone to fill in for me so you don't have to see me. If this is what you want, if you want to end this between us," he shakes his head, "then I'll stay out of your way. But keep the job."

I stare at him before nodding slowly. *Of course he's so thoughtful about everything, of course he offers me more than I deserve.*

"Is this really what you want?" he asks quietly.

I nod again.

He stands, his features shadowed by a heaviness, a betrayal that feels like a punch to my stomach.

"Okay." He exits my bedroom without looking back, as if he can't bear to see me. Moments later, the door to my apartment closes with a finality that shatters me.

I bend over at the waist, a keening sound escaping my lips, as tears erupt out of me.

"Emma," Cassie's voice is quiet as she climbs next to me in bed and pulls me into her arms.

She holds me tightly while I cry. For too many hours to count.

22

LUKE

I slept like shit.

Thoughts of Emma, the sound of her voice, the meaning of her words kept me up all night. Now it's 9:00 AM and I'm pacing around my kitchen, still trying to make sense of the crap Emma said to me yesterday. Even my morning run did nothing to calm my mind. If anything, I'm even more amped up now than I was last night.

"He's behind this." I bang the bottom of my fist against the countertop, desperate to put it through a wall instead.

"You don't know that," Gray replies.

"Are you fucking kidding me? It makes no goddamn sense!" I explode at him, his calm demeanor pissing me off even more.

"Neither does jumping to conclusions. Luke, I know it's easy to blame my dad. I do it all the time. But you can't assume it's him just because she looked weird when you mentioned him. Have you ever considered that maybe, just maybe, she doesn't want to try a long-distance thing and wants to keep whatever's between you guys here in DC?"

"No."

"Dude, think it through."

"I have." I point a finger at him. "Your dad is behind this, and I'm going to figure out what the hell he's pulling."

Gray sighs heavily. "Alright, what can I do to help?"

"Just keep an eye on her." My fingers grip the underside of the countertop as I rock back and forth. "Make sure she's okay."

"Of course."

"I've got to get to the gym."

"You're still going?"

"Yeah. I made a commitment. And I could use the distraction."

"Alright dude, I'll head to the restaurant. See about hiring another server."

"Thanks, Gray." I slap him on the shoulder as I lift my gym bag and leave my apartment.

The cold air feels good against the heat rushing over my skin every time I think of Emma, the blank expression on her face, the harshness of her words.

Ducking into the gym, I'm desperate to block everything out and lose myself in a good brawl. My fingers itch to call Toby to set up a fight, to go bare knuckles with some wannabe.

"Who wants in the ring?" I call out to the gym at large, as I kick my bag into a corner. "Anyone?" I turn around, my arms flung out wide beside me.

A hush settles over the gym as the guys scattered around, engaged in various exercises, pause to look at me, to exchange looks with each other.

"Come on."

"Man." Manny comes up next to me, placing a hand on my shoulder that I shake off. "What's going on?"

"I just need to fight. And I'm not dialing Toby, I'm here. So someone fight me." I raise my voice at the last part.

"Suit up then." A deep voice says behind me.

Turning around, my eyebrows raise in surprise when I see Scoop leaning against the doorjamb of Frankie's office.

"For real?"

"Yeah. It's about time you try to take a shot at me."

I laugh, but the sound is unsteady. Digging into my gym bag, I pull out my wraps and gloves. Popping in my mouth guard, I step into the ring and wait for Scoop.

Manny shakes his head at me. "Sure about this?"

"Yeah."

When Scoop enters the ring… I can't explain it but somehow, the air charges, the energy changes, the silence that descends on the gym is strange. Something is off. I'm pretty sure it's me. In the corner, I catch Frankie's eye. He shakes his head at me, disappointed, before disappearing into his office.

Manny calls Scoop and me to the center and has us tap gloves. Ramos rings the bell. And here I am, fighting one of my idols. For a moment, admiration bubbles in my chest and my inner eleven-year-old shouts with excitement.

Then Scoop cuts a jab across the right side of my face and all nostalgia disappears.

Putting my gloves up to shield my face, I circle Scoop. He bounces lightly from foot-to-foot, his eyes narrowed in on me.

I throw out a jab to test him but he blocks it easily, a strange smile crossing his face.

Screw this. I'm not going to play it safe. I'm hyped up in a swell of anger so large, it could drown me. Shutting down all thoughts, I hone in on my technique, on the physicality of boxing, on the peace that fighting provides me with.

Then I unleash on Scoop.

Jab, jab, cross. Jab, cross, hook.

We clinch. Manny pulls us apart.

"Impressive," Scoop spits out. "Now that I know you're for real, I'll stop going easy on you."

"Give me your best."

He nods, anticipation for the challenge glinting in his dark eyes. He comes at me with a series of jabs. Some I deflect, some he lands. But then he throws an overhand punch, a corkscrew, that cuts me right across the right cheek, splitting the skin. "Come on, Luke. This is your best? How're you going to do against Lightning?"

I shake my head, throwing out a wild punch which Scoop easily ducks.

"Focus," he demands. "Rule your anger. Don't let it rule you."

I spit. He laughs.

Jab, jab. I catch him in the abdomen and he hisses out a breath before catching me again on the chin. I stagger back and he's on me, working me against the ropes, landing blow after blow.

The fight goes out of me, the anger bleeding from my pores like open wounds.

"Get your hands up."

I grin instead.

He lands a few more blows but he's pulling his punches, not trying to knock me out, just trying to knock some sense into me.

After a few more moments, he drops his hands, stepping back. "You good?"

I nod.

"Sure?"

I suck my lips into my mouth, biting down hard. "Yeah, man."

"You have strength and conditioning today. Better hit the weights." He climbs out of the ring.

The energy in the ring deflates, the usual noise and general sounds of the gym resume.

I stand for a few more minutes, staring at nothing.

"Luke." Frankie's gruff voice catches me off guard and breaks the spell of silence I'm stuck in.

I turn around to look at him, leaning against the ropes behind me.

"Hey, Frankie."

"Whatever it is that's eating you, use it. Use it to help you focus, to be more committed, more dedicated. Not as an excuse to act like a reckless, stupid kid. Today, you walked into my gym looking for a fight because you're hopped up on anger. I don't stand for that shit. Never have. You know better." He sighs, wiping a hand along his brow. "Whoever she is, she's got you twisted in knots. Maybe she's worth it if she can get to you like this." He smiles at that, as if he's enjoying seeing me tangled up and stupid. "But there isn't room for her in my gym. So leave her outside, leave it all outside, and come in here to train. To win. Got me?"

"Yeah, Frankie. I got you."

"Scoop went easy on you. I would've knocked you the fuck out for tossing out a challenge like that." He smacks me upside the head before handing me a tissue. "Get cleaned up before you bleed on the canvas."

I climb out of the ring and press the tissue to my cheek to stop the bleeding. Pulling a bottle of water and earbuds from my gym bag, I select a random playlist from Spotify and walk over to the weights to lift. Focusing on every rep, I'm grateful when the noise in my head quiets down.

It isn't until later that I realize Frankie and Scoop watched me the entire time. Really watched me. Like I'm more than just some boxer to them. Like they care. Like I'm one of theirs. And maybe in some way, I am.

23

EMMA

*G**ray: Stop being a little brat.***
Ignoring Gray's message, I scour the government website for jobs I'm eligible for.

Who needs Capitol Hill?

Why am I putting all my eggs in one basket anyway?

There are other opportunities in DC than working on the Hill.

Right?

I open a job description for an NGO on M street. Scanning the requirements, I click out of it once I see that an advanced degree is required.

Jeez, how are young people supposed to find employment these days?

I sigh, scrolling through various postings, my eyes frantic for a position I can fulfill.

My phone chimes again.

I still my search and sit, debating if I should look at the screen or not.

I called out of work the past three days. By work, I mean both my internship and Barracuda. I'm officially eating ramen. Silver lining: I've lost three pounds since Sunday.

It's Wednesday.

My fingers itch to flip my phone back over. Part of me desperately wishes Luke's name will appear in the message box. The other part of me dreads any mention of him.

Is this heartbreak? This empty, desolate feeling of hope and dread and nausea?

I cave and pick up my phone.

Gray: Answer me, Stanton.

I place the phone back down.

Pushing my hair behind my ears, I stare at my computer screen. Maybe if I stare long enough, my dream job will jump out at me.

A knock at the door jars me from my staring.

"Cass, can you get that?"

Moments pass and the knock sounds again.

Oh, right. It's Wednesday. 2:00 PM. Obviously, Cassie is at work like a normal person. Not sitting in her room in ratty sweats bemoaning life.

Sighing, I force myself to answer the door. "What are you doing here, Gray?"

"Wow, Stanton. You look like shit."

"Thanks."

He pushes past me into my apartment and looks around. "Nice place. Not really the color palette I would have envisioned for you, but good for temporary housing."

"What do you want, Gray?"

His eyes cut to me. "That's it? What do I want?"

I close the door and face him, crossing my arms over my chest and widening my eyes for him to explain.

"God, Stanton. I want to make sure you're okay. Is that alright with you?" Gray's eyes flash with a spark of anger that is so out of character for him, it has me standing up straighter. He tugs on the back of his neck and shakes his head at me, disappointed. "Is it so terrible that you have people, friends, that care about you and are worried about you and want to check on you? Quit acting like a weirdo and just tell me, or better yet, tell Luke what's going on so we can help you fix it. And so that you can come back to work, because right now I'm really bored and I didn't peg you for selfish, Stanton."

I snort at his little quip but inside, his honesty hollows out a pit of guilt and warmth in my stomach. Guilt, because he's right. I do have friends; I do have people who care about me. And I've been blowing them off. Hardcore. Warmth because... well, the fact that he considers himself one of the people in that group is sweet and endearing. I've missed Gray. A lot. Not nearly as much as I miss Luke but still...

"You're right."

He takes a step back, a scowl marring his features for an instant. "Is this some reverse psychology you're trying to pull on me, Stanton? You're supposed to stand here and argue with me, picking at old wounds until we have a full out fight during which time you unload all your anger and hurt and whatever the hell else is bothering you. After that, I give you a hug, bribe you with a lot of ice cream, and go back to Luke and tell him everything you said so he can win you back."

Oh. My. What?

"Luke sent you here?"

"No, he's got too much pride. But that doesn't mean I won't try to help him any way I can. He's miserable, Stanton. And if you consider how cranky he is on a good day... he's going to lose business if he doesn't quit scowling at everyone. I mean, I can only do so much." He looks down at his shoes, scuffing his toe against the tile for a moment. "What happened?" Gray's eyes meet mine and his genuine concern causes tears to swell in my eyes.

"Shit." Gray pulls me into a hug.

I proceed to cry onto his shoulder, my tears staining his very expensive T-shirt. No wonder it's so soft against my cheek. It probably costs more than my rent.

"Emma?"

I wipe my eyes with the backs of my knuckles and drag the back of my hand across my nose.

"Attractive."

Pulling in a deep breath and tucking my knotty hair behind my ears, I look him square in the face and tell him the truth. "It's your dad."

Gray's eyebrows disappear into his hairline. I know I've surprised him.

"Go on." He urges, his voice hard. I'm not sure whether that hardness is directed at me or at his father but at this point, all I can do is tell him the truth.

So I do.

I tell him all of it. I tell him about the invitation to lunch, confiding in Senator Harrington about my desire to work on the Parental Leave issue, the bill he proposed to co-sponsor with LeBeau, his insistence that I take point on research. I tell him about his dad's bribe to help me find a job on the Hill if I convince Luke to drop the fight in December. I tell him about the warning that Luke could be injured. And finally, Harrington's threat to pull the legislation if I don't break it off with Luke completely.

Confessing this part has me hiccupping and snorting in the most obnoxious combination ever. I wish the floor would open up and pull me through all the way to the level of molten lava.

"Relax, Emma." Gray circles my wrist and pulls me into

my living room. We sit on the couches and stare into the space between us.

Finally, Gray gets up and rummages around my kitchen. He returns with a bottle of tequila and some shot glasses and I realize in that moment that Gloria Stanton would be horrified. I never even offered Gray a drink.

"Take this." He pushes a shot in my direction.

I toss it back, wincing at the sting.

He takes a shot as well. "We need alcohol for this."

I nod in agreement. I would have started drinking weeks ago if I knew I was going to end up here.

"So my dad is pretty much threatening to kill a piece of legislation that you really care about and that will help millions of people if you don't stop seeing Luke?"

"That about sums it up."

"So you tried to break up with Luke?"

"I did break up with Luke."

"It doesn't count if you don't mean it."

I smile at him, a tear sliding down my cheek. *Oh my God. Get it together, Emma.*

Gray reaches out and stops the tear with his forefinger. "Emma, I'm going to tell you something that's probably going to break your heart a little bit more."

I inhale deeply, suddenly scared. I don't know if I can take any more hurt this week.

"My dad was never going to help pass that legislation."

"What?" Confusion rocks through me as I try to process his words. "No Gray, I heard LeBeau on the phone talking to him and –"

"Sure, he was going to talk to LeBeau about it and get the ball rolling. But in no way was he going to throw his weight behind that issue. He doesn't care enough about it. It's a good issue, not crazy controversial, something he can use to help bolster his campaign message to the Democrats in the months to come but nothing he was going to outright champion. He would let LeBeau take the lead on that and provide support here and there."

Gray shrugs. "He wanted you on the issue because he knew you would pour your heart into it and it would give him leverage over you. And it did. He was going to help you find a job, work on more issues you care about, have a career on The Hill in exchange for convincing Luke to back out of the fight." He snickers. "I bet his eyes bulged from his face when you shot him down. No one shoots him down. Ever."

I manage a snort.

"The threat of dropping the legislation if you end things with Luke is probably just out of spite. Because you didn't go along with what he wanted. He doesn't have the type of power to completely kill the legislation. I mean, he does, but it would take a lot more effort than he's willing to put in. Trust me."

"So I broke up with Luke for nothing?"

"It would appear that way. The legislation," he looks at me with sadness in his cocoa eyes, "that was never about you at all."

I wince at the realization that I was played as I pick at a hole in the knee of my sweatpants. Not my finest hour.

"Why does your Dad want Luke to drop out of the fight? Boxing is his dream."

Gray sighs, crossing his right ankle over his left knee and leaning back in the chair. He rests his head back and contemplates my question. I continue picking at the hole, watching as it grows larger. I should probably throw these pants out.

Gray passes me another shot of tequila. We both drink. We both wince.

"You don't have any lemons or limes or even an orange to chase this with?" He drops his glass back on the coffee table.

"I only have ramen. And coffee. Want a coffee?"

"No thanks. Don't tell Luke that. He'll lose his mind if he thinks you're really only eating ramen noodles like some poor college kid."

"First off, Luke and I aren't talking, so that's a moot point. Secondly, I *am* a poor college kid."

"No need to draw extra attention to that fact."

"Whatever. Tell me about your dad. I'm not even following at this point." I hold my shot glass out and swing it back and forth until Gray pours me some more tequila. It's definitely going straight to my head, what with the lack of food in my stomach to soak it up, but for some reason, it feels really good to be reckless after so many weeks of being disciplined.

Glancing down again, I note my holey sweats and stained T-shirt. My unwashed hair and bare feet. The fact that it's Wednesday afternoon and I'm sitting on my couch drinking Cassie's tequila with Gray after very responsibly calling out of work with the flu. Cough, sneeze. Okay, fine, I wouldn't call this reckless either. Immature? Perhaps. Thoughtless? Nah, I can't seem to turn my thoughts or emotions off. Capricious? Yes, capricious then.

It feels really good to be capricious.

"Emma?" Gray snaps his fingers, bringing me back to my living room with the lacking color palette.

"Hm?"

"Whatever my dad's reasons are for wanting Luke to drop out of the fight, I'm sure it's something to do with money, reputation, or control. He's planning to announce for the Republican Presidential bid next year. If I had to guess, it has something to do with that. But trust me, it really isn't about you."

We share a laugh at that.

"Come on. We need to go see Luke."

"What? Why?" Panic seizes my heart. *I can't see Luke looking like this.*

Gray hunches forward, resting his elbows on his knees. "Relax, you can shower and not look like… this." He waves his hand in my direction, a strange expression crossing his face. "In fact, I insist that you shower."

I stick my tongue out at him.

"Ah, she's still in there, folks. Welcome back, Stanton."

I flip him the bird. He grins.

"Do you really think your dad would want Luke to give up his lifelong dream because of his plans to announce his campaign bid?" Preston Harrington the Third would be a horrible president. I mean, he wants to ruin the dreams of his family members before he even holds office. Not a good sign.

Gray sighs, getting comfortable in the chair again. "Emma, this city is not for you. Let me correct that. This city *is* for you because Luke is here and you can do all these things your wild about. But politics is not for you. You're too sweet."

"It's starting to appear that way, isn't it?

"Go shower. You're gross."

I blink at him. Knowing that I am in fact a bit tipsy and a shower can only help matters, I oblige. Stalling will give me time to sort out what to say to Luke. How to desperately beg for his forgiveness.

24

LUKE

Tossing the bar towel down, I rake my fingers through my hair. I'm so tired, I'm weary. It's a different kind of exhaustion than the one that plagues my muscles after a fight or a late night out. This strain of exhaustion is crippling, and I want nothing more than to blow everything off, grab a bottle of Jack, drink it all, and sleep. For a long, long time.

The scrape of the door against the floor forces my eyes up. "Our kitchen opens back up at 5:00PM."

"How about drinks?" she asks, her voice low like a punch to the gut.

"Becca?"

"Hey, baby." She sashays closer, flipping her long auburn hair over her shoulder. She leans over the bar, expertly pushing her cleavage closer to my chest as she runs her fingertips over my cheek and kisses the corner of my mouth. "Missed you."

I close my eyes, recalling the time we spent together months ago in New York. A week of wild nights and lazy days. A series of parties and debauchery. We had fun. A lot of fun. And then I sobered up, came home, visited Uncle Steve's grave, and forgot all about the darkest week of my life.

But apparently, Becca was here to remind me.

Her mouth travels over mine for the briefest of seconds before I step back. "You're here?"

Her eyes flick up to mine and a slow smile crosses her lips. She's as hot as ever. Long hair, tight body, full pout. But it doesn't have the same effect this time. Now, she seems too skinny, almost strung out, tired in a way that has nothing to do with sleep.

"Who the hell are you?"

My neck snaps up, my eyes searching for Gray. Instead, they land on the shattered face of Emma, her beautiful eyes bleeding with pain, her bottom lip trapped between her teeth.

Fuck.

I feel the flash of guilt cross my face even though I'm not sure what I'm guilty of. I know immediately how this looks and I don't like it. I don't like hurting Emma. Watching the confusion in her eyes ebb into a sadness so large, it's a tidal wave. I step around the side of the bar, ignoring Becca completely.

"Em," I take a step toward her, my arm outstretched.

She shakes her head, as if coming out of a daze. "Excuse me." she whispers quietly, politely. Then she turns on her heel and disappears out the door.

Gray glares at me before glancing at Becca with disgust. Dismissing us both, he follows my girl out the door and leaves me standing alone, with the shadow of my past hovering behind me.

I grip the back of my neck before turning toward Becca. "What are you doing here?"

"I missed you."

"You don't even know me. Why are you here? What do you want?"

Her eyes fill with tears but oddly enough, they have no effect on me. Becca is a fun girl. Practically a professional. She knows how to turn the waterworks on and off at a moment's notice. "I thought we had something special, Luke." She shrugs one shoulder and I'm struck by how bony it is. "I thought we could see where things go." She walks over to me, trailing her hands up my abdomen, my chest. I place my hands over hers, stopping their trek.

"If that was true, you wouldn't have waited so many months to seek me out. Why are you really here?"

She huffs, turning away to hoist herself up on the bar, her feet dangling. "I hear you're fighting Lightning in December."

"Yeah."

"It's a couple hundred grand."

"Ah, you're here for a payday, are you?"

"Luke, come on, it's not like that between us. I just thought," she shrugs, "I could help take the edge off while you're training. And then, when you win, we could, be together."

"So you want to be my," I furrow my eyebrows, "prostitute?" The word is out of my mouth before I can swallow it back and I wince, closing my eyes and dropping my head back. Fine, I don't hold a great deal of respect for the fangirls. I've seen how they act around guys, around money, around the general boxing culture. This situation with Becca is a perfect example. But I hold myself to a higher standard, at least I want to. Saying that to Becca, even though it's the truth, was a low blow. I wish I could take the words back but they're out now, floating in the air between us. "Becca, I'm sorry." I place a hand on her arm and will her to look at me. "That was uncalled for and I shouldn't have said it."

"No," she shakes her head. "I guess you're right. I mean, the only reason guys want me is for sex anyway." She takes a deep breath. "But you were so nice to me, Luke. So good. We had such a fun time together. Do you remember?" She leans forward, her hand circling around my wrist, her eyes focused on mine. "Things were so easy between us. It could be like that again. Don't you want a smooth, drama-free girl to come home to at night?" She drops her head and brushes her lips over mine.

I stiffen.

Why the hell am I listening to this lying fangirl when I should be out searching for my real girl?

"Cut the crap, Becca. New York was months ago, and it meant nothing. You need to leave. Now." I hustle her off the bar and toward the door. "Don't show your face here again." I close the door behind her and bang my head against the wood.

Damn it!

Why was Emma even here?

And how much worse did I make things between us?

25

EMMA

S he was beautiful. One of the most beautiful girls I've ever seen and that's saying something since Lila is my best friend.

She was tall and graceful. And so, so skinny. Her clothes hugged all the right curves. Her hair was a reddish-brown that would be impossible to imitate. Her eyes were green and sparkling. Like the emeralds in my Pretty Pretty Princess set that I wore as a five-year-old.

She was pretty like a princess.

Suddenly, I wish I never changed out of my holey, stinky sweats because right now I need them like a toddler needs a security blanket.

"Emma." Gray's voice is low beside me.

I look up at him, completely sober now that I've witnessed Luke with a beautiful girl pressed against him. I should have drunk more. *Who the hell wants to be sober in a moment like this?* Obviously, I'm going to call out of work again tomorrow. I probably won't even have to lie at this point. I bet I do wake up incredibly ill in the morning. With a stomach virus. From a night of heavy drinking.

"Who is she?" I ask, hating that my voice sounds as weak and fragile as I feel. Like a large gust of wind could break me in half.

"I don't know." He sounds disappointed and I know he is telling the truth. "Obviously, a fangirl. Probably someone he hooked up with a while back."

"Probably."

"Want to get a drink?" Gray asks, tossing an arm over my shoulder and pulling me into his side.

I'm about to agree when I remember that I'm already behind on my rent payment. Oh my God. I'm too poor to drink. This is how people probably end up homeless. I'm going to be homeless.

"Let me take you for a drink," Gray amends.

We turn into the next open bar we pass and I don't even flinch when I toss back the shot of tequila Gray nudges into my hand.

I vow to drink until I'm numb.

And Gray willingly agrees to keep the supply of alcohol flowing.

I'm two more shots and a beer down and the night starts to take on a comical color. In fact, I find the whole damn thing hysterical.

"I'm going to be homeless and unemployable," I tell Gray, my head bopping to the beat of a Calvin Harris track. "I love this song!"

"Homeless maybe, but I'm pretty sure you'll still be employable. I mean, you got the job at Barracuda with no relevant skills, so you'll be fine."

"I like that you always tell it like it is Gray. No fluff. Just straight shooting. You're a good friend."

"I try." He hunches forward on the bar ledge, keeping his head low.

"Avoiding anyone in particular or just embarrassed to be seen with me?"

"The blonde at three o'clock." He admits sheepishly. "Never called her after a night of liberal libations."

"Ah." I nod, blatantly turning my head to three o'clock.

She's gorgeous. Of course she is. She's tall and thin and stunning. Her jeans are slimming and frayed at the bottom. Her blouse is loose and flowy. Long blond hair cascades down her back and over her shoulders, thick like a mane. And I particularly like her moccasins.

"She's beautiful. You should call her."

"Why would I be embarrassed to be seen with you? I mean, the disgusting sweats, yes. But you're all cleaned up now."

I punch him in the arm, avoiding his question. I didn't mean to admit that little truth. Alcohol. Ugh.

"Let's have another round."

———

THE BAR IS SPINNING.

Literally.

Or maybe I'm spinning.

I'm dizzy in a delicious way and it makes me want to laugh. Raising my arms over my head, I continue twirling. Gray's face flashes before me as his arms reach out to clasp my waist and steady me.

"Take it easy, Stanton, or you'll be puking early."

I smile at him, closing my eyes and spreading my arms wide. I'm drunk as a skunk. Ah, I've missed this feeling in an awkward way. Nights like these, out dancing and drinking with Lila. Giggling as we attempted to sneak back into our apartment, trying desperately not to wake Mia and Maura. They were like our parents: responsible, disciplined, dedicated. And we were the unruly and reckless teenagers. A pang of nostalgia hits me in the chest, momentarily stealing my breath.

"I miss my friends."

"You have friends here too, Stanton."

"Sure," I say noncommittally. But as much as I like Gray, he could never be Lila, Mia, or Maura. They're like my sisters. Except I also have Daphne and Celia.

Celia! She's going to be uneducated and unemployable if I don't get my life back on track.

I gasp at this realization, my nostalgia replaced with horror as I realize that by blowing off both of my jobs this week, I've put Celia's future in jeopardy.

Worst. Sister. Ever.

"Are you going to puke?" Gray grabs my wrist and peers into my face.

I shake my head, my thoughts a jumbled mess.

"Promise?"

"I think I just got a reality check," I tell him honestly.

He shrugs, not understanding what I'm talking about. That's okay. I know what I'm talking about.

"Well, here comes another one."

"What?"

"Emma." The deep rasp of his voice jerks my eyes up while spreading goosebumps up and down my arms.

Luke.

I stare at him, my mouth ajar. My eyes swing to Gray and he holds his hands up in surrender.

"He's my cousin."

"I strike my comment about you being a good friend from the record."

He grins at me and disappears into the crowd on the dance floor. Leaving me.

Alone.

With Luke.

"Where's your friend?" My voice is edged with steel and I cringe at my obvious jealousy. I'm so freaking jelly it hurts.

Luke winces, stepping closer and gripping my hips.

I stare straight at the base of his neck. And even that nondescript part of his body is beautiful.

"Emma." His deep voice begs me to lift my eyes but I can't. I can't look at him because then I'll be reminded of all I lost.

I knew better!

I knew better than to fall for a guy like Luke. But I went ahead and started falling off a freaking cliff hoping he would catch me anyway. I hit the stupid pavement. Hard. And the stark realization that I could never be enough for him, that I'm not enough for him, smacked me right in the face. Josh McCannon and Luke could be besties.

"Emma," he repeats, his hands sliding up my ribcage before grabbing my wrists and tugging me against his chest. He wraps his arms around me and hugs me.

And I let him. I crumple into his chest like a tissue.

Because I'm weak. And sad. And a used tissue who just fell off a cliff.

"Emma. I miss you. A lot." he whispers into my hair. His words make me feel marginally better, but so could ice cream so I'm not caving just yet. "I swear, there's nothing going on between me and Becca."

I knew it! She would have a name like Becky. Or Becca. Whatever.

"I didn't know she was coming. There's nothing between us. Never was. She caught me by surprise, and I know things looked really bad but, Em, I swear, it's nothing." He pulls back to meet my eyes and the truth and sincerity I read in them nearly undoes me. Okay fine, it pulls at my heart strings and unravels some of my resistance but then I remember Josh McCannon. And his "not my type" comment. I know, deep down in my heart of hearts know, that I'm not Luke's type. So why keep going down this road?

This semester was supposed to be a growth opportunity for me to embrace new things, be brave, have an adventure. Instead, I've worked my ass off at two jobs with nearly nothing to show for it and fell off a cliff for a bad boy with a gash on his cheek and knuckle tattoos who is so much better suited for Becky the Twig. I've lost focus. I need to leave here in a month with a job lined up. I need to be serious and determined.

I can't keep being a stupid tissue.

Shaking my head, I swallow back the lump of tears that's traveling up my throat. "I believe you, Luke."

Relief washes over his features and a small smirk ticks up the left side of his mouth.

I pull my hand out of his grasp and hold it up before he gives me a full-out smile and makes the next words out of my mouth impossible.

"I believe you about Becca. But still, I can't do this."

"Why are you pulling away from me?" He steps closer, his breath fanning out over my cheek. "Things between us were going so great and then you just pulled away. Why? What happened?" He's so serious, so worried, that I want to jump into his arms and let him take me home with him and tuck me into his bed forever.

Stupid dreams.

"All of this is too much. I'm not made for your world. You and me, we were never going to go anywhere. Not really. Isn't it better this way? We pull off the Band-Aid before either one of us is in too deep?"

His eyes flick down to my mouth, where my lips are spouting off lies, and I work a swallow. I'm already in too deep and I'm pretty sure the entire freaking universe knows it.

"Emma, just let me try to understand. I –"

"I can't do this," I cut him off, knowing I need to get out of the bar before I start ugly crying. "We're not right for each other Luke. Seeing you with Becca, even if nothing happened, just reminded me of that. And I need to remember it. Good luck with your fight and with everything." I wave a general hand in his direction, having absolutely no idea what "everything" is supposed to entail. "Goodbye, Luke."

Then I turn on my heel and stride to the exit, half-stumbling, half-hiccupping, full-blown ugly crying the entire time.

I suck at the stupid pact.

SADNESS PLAGUES ME, making my limbs feel heavy. But after nearly two weeks of wallowing, so much so that I even missed Thanksgiving, I finally pull myself together. I throw out those dingy sweats. I take the longest shower in history, scrubbing the depressing scent of heartbreak from my skin. I clean my room, kind of. Then I spend some much-needed time in my closet putting together my outfits for the week. Even if I'm miserable, at least I'll look good. Right?

I've lost weight. Usually, this fact would elate me. But now... okay, it's still the silver lining. For one, because I lost weight. Secondly, no one will have a hard time buying my sick story at my internship. Solid.

Checking my account balance, I'm relieved to see that I've saved enough money for next month's rent. Forgoing my metro pass for next month, I decide to walk more so that I can keep saving money and continue my fitness journey.

Fitbit rules my life.

When Monday morning arrives, I will be a better version of myself. Or an older version. The one that was motivated, determined, focused.

#LifeGoals

26

LUKE

*W*e were never going to go anywhere.

Her voice plays over and over in my mind. Even when I close my eyes, I see her face, the sadness seeping into her eyes, the tears tracking her cheeks. Even when I work the heavy bag, I hear her words, the catch in her breath as she says them, the pain in her voice as she forces out a lie.

We were never going to go anywhere.

Or is it the truth?

I hit the bag again, letting it swing back at me. Moving from side to side, I focus on my footwork. I throw jab after jab after jab. The impact of my fist with the bag sends a jolt up my arm, into my shoulder. My knuckles crunch under the thin layer of tape I applied. The burn and sting feels so fucking good. It serves a purpose. It reminds me that this is my world. This is my life. And girls like Becca, they're the ones I'm supposed to kick it with.

We were never going to go anywhere.

Fuck. That hurt. Her words cut me deeper than all the cuts I've gotten stitches for in the past. Her words burned through me like fire, scorching a path of destruction that blazed bright before turning to ash.

Her words took away all the hope I was clinging to that I could fix the shit between us. That I could somehow understand why she pulled back. That I could still have her. Make her mine. Make her want to be mine.

We were never going to go anywhere.

And now I know the truth. Glossy girls like Emma, who have real educations and big dreams, who maintain morals over everything, who work for the betterment of others, could never settle for a brute like me. She'd hate the sketchy blurred lines of this life. The long stretches of training in other countries. The distance I'd be forced to put between us. Repeatedly. She would never be into a relationship for some exaggerated perks, like bragging rights. She'd want it all. She deserves it all.

And I never had it all together, to give, to begin with.

I grab the bag between my hands, stopping it's wild swinging. Resting my sweat-slicked forehead against the bag, I breathe out, close my eyes, and admit that she was right. Truthful.

We were never going to go anywhere.

I'M A MACHINE.

I've never been more singularly focused on anything in my life. Everything is scheduled. My wake-up time. When I hit the pillow at night. The food I eat. The workouts I repeat. Everything.

Barracuda is under the management of Gray. He runs everything, keeps inventory going, schedules staff, and oversees the day-to-day things that used to eat up all my time. I never thought a time would come when Gray emerged to shoulder a massive burden for me but he's doing it. And I'm grateful. Because of him and his commitment to Barracuda, I can commit all my time, all my energy, all of me to boxing. To the upcoming fight.

Now that I don't have to see her every day, breathe her in at night, thoughts of Emma fade into a memory. Sometimes I question if she was ever even real. She flutters through my mind from time to time, generally when I'm about to pass out from exhaustion or when I drag my insanely sore body from bed in the stupid early morning hours. Other than that, I block her out. Forget her beautiful smile, erase the way she fiddled with her bangs when she was nervous, shut off the sound of her laughter in my eardrums.

Right now, the only thing I can starve for is winning.

I'm at the gym seven days a week. Under the watchful eye of Scoop, my meals are monitored. Everything I consume is measured and portioned. The guys at the gym keep me in a strict rotation. Footwork, sparring, strength and conditioning, speed. They hone me into a better boxer, a stronger athlete, a fearsome contender.

I listen to all the advice given. I follow all the rules. I commit to the execution of every single punch I throw.

Above all, I stay starving.

DECEMBER

27

EMMA

"Hey."

"You're early," Gray grins at me from behind the bar.

I slide onto a barstool and gratefully accept a cup of coffee. "How's manager life treating you?"

"Ah, it's a natural fit for a natural charmer."

"I wish I was as modest as you, Gray."

"We'll get you there, Stanton. Hungry?"

I shake my head.

Over the last few weeks, Gray and I have settled into our routine. He doesn't bring up Luke, and I don't ask about him. Instead, we commiserate over other things: my lack of employment come June and money woes, his not-so-secret obsession with a mystery girl (it's the girl who works at the coffee house down the street), stupid jokes that no one else would laugh at, and the master plan of manipulation that his dad is scheming.

You know, normal things.

I'm grateful that Luke stepped back from life at the restaurant to focus on his boxing career. I want him to be happy and it seems like pursuing his dream is a really important step in achieving happiness. Selfishly, it means I don't have to see him, interact with him, or stare at him until I go blind and/or cry hysterically to him about how much I miss him. His absence makes the healing easier, faster. And I am healing. I'm focusing on other things – like job applications, catching up with my best girls and all the romantic things occurring in their lives.

If I'm being honest, I'm quite happy with the appearance I see in the mirror these days. The past few weeks of clean eating, walking everywhere (still not caving to buy that monthly metro card), and yoga two times a week with Cassie has helped sculpt my body into a leaner, stronger, healthier version. Plus, the yoga, in addition to giving Cassie and me a chance to hang out in our living room, has added a sense of peace and calmness to my life that was severely lacking. I feel good. No longer trying to be anyone's type but the best "type" for me, I'm happy to report that I'm at least accomplishing that goal.

"I think we're going to have a busy morning since it's supposed to snow next week."

"Ugh. I hate snow." I shake my head, sliding off the barstool. "I'll start setting up."

"Stanton?"

"Yeah?"

"His fight is next weekend. I've got an extra ticket in case you want to go."

Oh. I pause. Didn't see that coming. I mean, I knew his fight was next weekend, especially since Cassie keeps dropping hints. She's a lot less committed than Gray to the no-one-talk-about-Luke rule I tried to enforce. "Okay."

"No pressure. Just throwing it out there."

"Got it. Thanks Gray."

"I know it would mean a lot to him if you were there."

I freeze, my back to him. *Would Luke care if I was there? Does he want me to go?*

The old wounds of my heart sting in my chest. Healing schmealing.

Nodding once, I disappear into the kitchen to grab a stack of menus and rolled silverware.

Do I want to watch Luke's fight?

Desperately. I want to support him so badly, I don't even care if he knows I'm there. I just want to cheer him on and feel insane amounts of pride that he's living his dream.

Except, the mere thought of watching Luke get punched in the face makes me want to puke.

Repeatedly.

Deciding to table this inner monologue for the time being, I'm grateful for the brunch rush that takes Barracuda by storm, allowing me to disappear into work mode for several hours.

***

"ADD HEMP HEARTS." Cassie reminds me as I blend us smoothies after our yoga practice the following evening.

Luke's match is in five days. I still haven't decided if I'm going. Cassie keeps offering to go with me, but I'm still on the fence.

I add a scoop of hemp hearts and power up the blender. Pouring our green smoothies into glasses, I follow Cassie back into the living room where we curl up on the couch and get ready for the newest episode of *Outlander*.

Settling back against the cushions, I'm so ready to lose myself in the delicious drama and true love of Jamie and Claire for the next hour. Now that Cassie and I have traded in our wine glasses for smoothies, I'm adding another check next to my new healthy lifestyle. And growing bank account.

When Gray took over managing Barracuda, he agreed to give me all the shifts I could take on. And then he didn't hire another waitress even though the crowds almost demanded it. Instead, he told me to step up my game and take all the tables. After a few overwhelming nights where I may have forgotten to breathe, I settled in. A huge thanks to Hector, Raoul, and Jorge for their patience and encouragement. A big hug to Gray for putting me in an impossible situation. And a happy dance for me who now has saved enough money for the next few months of rent.

Budgeting sucks, but feeling like an adult is sort of cool. Sometimes.

"So, let's discuss outfits for Friday night," Cassie throws out, as if I already agreed to attend Luke's fight.

"Shh, it's about to start."

Cassie glances at her phone. "We still have three minutes. Don't deflect. We're going, right? I mean, we have to go. You're partially responsible for encouraging him to go after his dream anyway."

"What are you chattering about?"

She bites back a smile, tucking her feet underneath her.

Two minutes.

"Gray told me Luke was all set on running his family's restaurant and forgetting all about boxing until you told him about your goals for after graduation. Apparently, you inspired him with your passion for all of your causes." She waves a hand dismissively, as if that part isn't important at all. "After one of your fiery speeches on family leave, he decided to give boxing another go."

Oh. Hm. I didn't know that.

"And then, when you broke his heart, he committed to the

sport even more, giving 100% of his focus to this crazy fight that you have to be at because it's important to him."

"I didn't break his heart." Of course I pick the most obvious slight, just as she intended.

One minute.

Cassie settles me with a stare.

"He broke mine too."

"I know, Emma. You guys hurt each other because you both care about each other a stupid amount and are scared and uncertain about your future. But who isn't? You like him, Em. You like him a lot. And instead of just owning that and seeing where it could lead, you backed out because you didn't want to get hurt. I get that. I really do." She nods to emphasize her point. "But wasn't your whole pact or promise or whatever with your friends to make this semester about taking chances and pushing past your comfort zone?" She raises an eyebrow. "I promise you, with the way that boy looks at you, you weren't taking that big a risk."

Thirty seconds.

"All I'm saying is if Claire and Jamie can defy time and space and all of the crazy obstacles that they are up against, like real things that they can't change, then you and Luke can give what's between you a real shot. Especially now that you're chasing your dreams and he's fighting for his. Why can't you guys chase and fight for each other? Okay, I'm done. It's starting." She reaches over me to grab the remote and increase the volume as the greatest book turned TV show ever begins.

After everything that happened, would Luke let me catch him? And would he fight to keep me?

"Fine. We'll go to the fight."

"Shh."

28

EMMA

"Excuse me? Emma?" A soft voice says behind me.

I whirl around and suck in a deep breath. It's her. The beautiful Becky.

"Can I help you?" I ask politely, my arms full with a stack of menus. I'm tempted to tell her to take a seat anywhere but I know she's not here to eat and I can't fake it.

She looks down briefly before meeting my gaze. Her bright eyes are sharp but open, her long hair falling around her shoulders. She smiles and it seems genuine. Damn it. I don't want to like her. *Don't like her, Emma!*

"I'm Becca." Becca, Becky, whatever.

"Hi." I fail already and smile at her. Ugh. Sometimes being nice sucks. Nice guys finish last and all that.

"Look, I just wanted to apologize to you. You seem like a really nice girl and I saw the way Luke was looking at you the other night." She fiddles with the strap of her purse, her fingers flicking the zipper back and forth nervously.

Say what? This I did not see coming. *And, more importantly, how was Luke looking at me the other night?*

"There's nothing between us," she continues. "It was

stupid of me to come here. Desperate even." She shrugs, offering an apologetic smile. "But I didn't mean to cause any trouble between you two."

"Thank you. For saying all of that. But you didn't ruin anything between us. Would you like something to eat?" I offer. Once I move past the part where she's a tiny little dancer with long hair and big eyes, I can objectively note that she looks exhausted, almost too-thin (does such a thing exist?), and skittish.

"Yeah, that'd be great. Thank you."

I gesture to the closest table and she takes a seat. Handing her a menu, I scuttle off to grab her a glass of water while she decides what to order.

It's quiet in the restaurant. A Thursday at 5:18 PM. Gray is coming in at 7:00 PM when things start to pick up with the dinner rush. For now, it's just me and Becca.

"What will it be?" I place down her water glass.

"Cajun chicken wrap with fries." She hands the menu back to me.

"Anything else to drink?"

"Nope."

I'm about to turn around to punch in her order when she places a hand on my arm. A very delicate hand with a fresh coat of nail polish. I clench my fingers into fists, hiding my chipped nails. There was a time when I never left the house without making sure my makeup was on point, my nails perfect, my outfit a reflection of the latest trend. Now, my hair is a frizzy mess pulled into a low ponytail and my nails are sporting a ten-day-old coat of Essie's "skirting the issue." Story of my life.

"Thank you. For being so nice to me." Her eyes well up with tears and I want to drop into the chair across from her and demand that she spill her guts. Fortunately, I get a grip.

She dabs at her eyes with the corner of a napkin. "I didn't expect you to be so nice. I hope you and Luke work things out."

"Thank you. I'll just put your order in."

She nods, pulling out her iPhone and tapping on her screen. Probably checking Facebook and Instagram.

I punch in her order and try to keep myself busy by rolling silverware, but my eyes keep flitting back to her. Something is off, but I can't place it. Becca sits at her table, still on her phone, but she's sitting too straight, too formal. Her eyes keep drifting to the clock as if she's waiting for someone to meet her here, but she didn't mention it. In fact, she didn't say much of anything other than the apology.

Well, what was I expecting? The girl to tell me her life story? Although I'm interested in the bit about her and Luke.

"Shit." she says suddenly, her voice carrying in the empty room. She glances up at me, a sheepish expression on her face. "I hate to ask you this." She waves her iPhone around before dropping it back in her purse. "But my phone just died. Do you think I could borrow yours really quick? My ride back to New York is on his way and I was just texting him the name of the restaurant so he could pick me up."

"Sure." I walk over and pass her my phone.

She smiles and slips outside to make the call.

Why couldn't she just tell her ride the address while sitting at her table?

I pop into the kitchen to collect her chicken wrap from Jorge.

"Here you go, Pequeña." He hands me the plate. "Anyone else out there?" He juts a chin toward the doors to the dining area.

"Nope, just table two."

"Then I'm gonna run up the street and grab a pack of cigarettes."

I frown.

"You'll be okay on your own for a few, right?"

"Of course." I swat at him. "You shouldn't be smoking!"

"You sound like my moms, Chica."

"Well, at least she tried to teach you something."

He laughs again, patting my head like a puppy. "I'll be right back. Need anything?"

"Nah, I'm good."

"Okay." Jorge slips out the back door.

I walk into the dining room and drop Becca's plate off at her table, but she's still gone. The restaurant is suddenly eerily quiet, and a shiver skirts up my arms. *What could be taking so long?* The thought that she jacked my phone runs through my mind before I shut it down. No need to judge the girl. Maybe she's having some issues with her ride.

I head back to the bar, back to my silverware rolling, back to my pathetic attempts at distraction. I make a pit stop at the bathroom, take some extra time to fix my ponytail.

Three more minutes pass and I start to feel wary.

Something is off.

Heading outside, I look for Becca.

Eighth Street is busy, with people leaving work, heading to happy hour, going home. People pass by, their heads bent low against the wind, cell phones attached to their hands and ears.

"Becca?" I call out, my eyes scanning for her.

This is bizarre.

Shivering against the cold, I hug myself, walking a few shops up the street. A strange noise stops me, and I turn toward the alley that leads to the back of the shops and restaurants. *Did something happen to her?*

Before I can think through all the reasons why walking into an alley, even in the dusky time before sunset, isn't a stellar idea, I hurry down the narrow path. "Becca?"

There's that sound! A mewling, almost like a kitten. Maybe it is a stray kitten and she needs milk. Or adoption. Maura would shoot me for being so naive.

My steps quicken. Before I can fully grasp the scene unfolding before me, a big hand wraps around my throat from behind, pulling me flush against a torso of solid muscle. Another hand covers my mouth.

"You're too easy to catch, love," the voice whispers in my ear, a mixture of accents I can't place given the circumstance. "I'll move my hand but if you scream, I'll hurt you." He squeezes the back of my neck roughly before dropping his hand from my mouth.

Becca steps out from the shadows, her eyes hard. "Sorry, Emma." She waves apologetically before turning toward another guy. "I did my bit." She holds out a hand and the guy hands her an envelope with what I presume is cash. Then she cuts on her heel and walks back toward Eighth Street, dismissing me as easily as cigarette ash.

My breath is stuck in my throat, which is closing at a rapid rate as I try not to hyperventilate. I'm frozen. Frozen in shock. But I'm quickly thawing into full-out panic mode.

"Don't move." The voice whispers again and I squeeze my eyes shut tight in a desperately lame attempt of "if I can't see it, then it must not be real."

"Who are you?"

The man holding me snorts. "Let's get moving." He nudges me forward toward a waiting van. He sounds almost cheerful, which is an entirely different kind of warning. He's enjoying this.

I follow along after that, my mind shutting down from all thoughts except the most important one: survival.

"There are people who will wonder where I am. I mean, I'm in the middle of a shift," I whisper to his large frame behind me as he shuffles me forward, closer to the van. The guy who gave Becca the cash is already in the driver's seat, his eyes hidden behind dark sunglasses.

Fingers tighten on the back of my neck. "That's the whole point, Princess."

All the breathing techniques I've been practicing during yoga fly right out the window as I try not to die from a lack of oxygen. I look down, counting my steps for no other reason than it's comforting. Plus, I'm scared I may trip and get accidentally shot or stabbed or whatever kidnappers do to their victims.

We're only a couple of feet away from the van now. I wrack my brain for everything I learned during an Oprah episode years ago about what to do if you're kidnapped. One girl managed to unplug the brake lights from the trunk she was stuffed into and the car that held her was pulled over by the police and she was saved! *Was there anything regarding vans?* I can't remember. *Think, Emma!*

"This is her?" A gruff voice causes me to look up in alarm.

Suddenly appearing, as if out of thin air, are two men dressed in dark clothing. Their beards hide the lower portions of their faces and dark sunglasses and hats keep other features concealed. They stir inside the van casually, as if this is a normal Thursday for them and they're just in the midst of sorting out who's bringing the beer.

My entire body trembles with chills. And adrenaline. And fear.

Mostly fear.

"Yes," the voice behind me confirms.

One of the guys tilts his head as he stares at me from behind his tinted shades.

"You sure he'll go for this?"

"That's what I hear."

"We'll see."

I lick my lips. My mouth is so dry I'm convinced it's cracked. "What's going on?" I ask, my eyes wildly searching around for Becca, who is obviously long gone. Ride to New York, my ass. That saying, "Better the devil you know than the devil you don't" floats through my head and I fight down the irrational urge to laugh. Because I don't even know Becca. Not at all. And yet, her presence would bring me comfort in this moment.

I'm delusional.

The guy standing closest, who I'm going to call Lip Ring because he has one and I'm too overwhelmed to be creative, reaches out and closes a hand around my bicep. He pushes me forward into the open door of the van. I stumble to my knees.

"Easy." The bulky man, who shall now be called Muscle, behind me is suddenly breathing on my neck. Heavily. I squirm, feeling bile rise in my throat. Are they going to…?

Muscle yanks me to my feet and nudges me farther into the van. Into the black abyss that awaits. He climbs in behind me, and although I can make out his large stature and tattooed hands in my peripheral vision, I'm too chicken to raise my head and take a peek.

"Sit down." Muscle's voice is low and gruff.

I quickly collapse into the nearest bucket seat as adrenaline leaks from my body. My legs transform from the formidable pillars that held me up on all thirty-three steps to the van into spaghetti noodles as soon as I'm seated.

"Place your hands on the arm rests, palms down." Lip Ring climbs in and crouches next to my seat, pulling a couple of zip ties from his pocket.

I know my eyes are bulging out of my head.

Oh. My. God. I'm a prisoner! At the mercy of men I don't know and can't even properly see all because of Becky Becca!

I do as he asks and watch as he ties my wrists to the arm rests.

Strangely enough, in this moment, all I feel is a surge of relief that I peed prior to leaving Barracuda. At least I won't have to think about my bladder for the next few hours and hopefully by then, I'll be free of this insane, terrifying situation.

"Close your eyes," Lip Ring continues, a bandana now in his hand. "Or don't." He shrugs, his hands reaching up and brushing errant strands of hair behind my ears.

I shudder, closing my eyes and shrinking away from his touch. Every single part of me goes on high alert. Suddenly, I'm truly terrified as to what these guys are going to do to me.

Am I going to show up on the news? Tied up, blindfolded, and dead?

"Relax," Lip Ring whispers to me. His hands continue pushing hair back from my face, his fingers lingering too long on the back of my neck and I stiffen.

Holy shit. They're going to rape me! My mind starts back up at the speed of light, suddenly imagining every single disgusting, horrible thing they can do to me. And here I sit, helpless to fight them off. Tears prick the corners of my eyes.

Lip Ring removes his hands. I feel the soft cloth of the bandana cover my eyes, wrap around the sides of my face and tighten at the back of my head as he ties it in a knot.

I sit quietly. Still. Focusing on the sound of my breathing.

Straining for any other noises that will alert me to their oncoming attack.

I'm so scared, so unbelievably fearful, that it takes me a moment to realize that the engine has started, and the van is moving. We're going somewhere.

Where the hell are we going?

I swallow loudly, trying to bolster my inner strength.

I'm okay. I'm okay. I'm okay.

But the opening bars of Guns N' Roses "Welcome to the Jungle" suddenly blaring from the speakers sounds way too ominous for me to believe my own lies.

———

TIME PASSES STRANGELY.

With each minute gone and each street corner cleared, I settle into my new state as prisoner. My body, exhausted from being stiff with fear, begins to relax and my mind wanders to other moments, random pieces of my life.

Daphne, Celia, Jon, and I opening gifts on Christmas morning.

Dancing in a summer rainstorm with Lila.

Hysterically laughing with my friends after a night out of drinking.

Hugging my dad.

The way Mom's sweaters always smell like honey and cinnamon.

Waking up next to Luke and being really, truly happy.

Jesus. I miss Luke. In this moment, I know that if he was here this entire scenario would be playing out differently. Tears well in my eyes, their moisture soaking into the bandana, their occurrence hidden from the eyes of the strangers around me.

I'm so going to die without ever telling Luke how I feel. Without ever really giving us a chance. Without ever really knowing what happens after you fall in love.

That thought makes the tears well up faster and I bite my lip hard to keep them from falling over. I need to get it together. I need to be strong. I need to survive.

We stop. The door scrapes open.

"You sure about this?" Muscle asks someone.

"Yeah, man. This will sort out all the issues with one quick fix." A voice I don't recognize responds from outside the van.

"I don't know." Lip Ring sounds hesitant, almost unsure.

My heart soars for the briefest of moments.

"Del Marco says she's a sure thing. He needs this situation wrapped up."

Del Marco. *Where do I know that name from?*

An awkward silence descends on the van. Several seconds of breathing and what I can only imagine of eye glancing and hand gesturing takes place around me.

"Whatever," Lip Ring reluctantly agrees to whatever just occurred.

My heart plummets once more.

Del Marco! Oh My God! Harrington's Chief of Staff?

What does he have to do with this?

Is Harrington behind this?

But I did what he asked! I ended things with Luke and emotionally destroyed myself.

How could he also have me kidnapped?

My mind is racing, trying to connect dots I'm not sure exist, trying to sort out a puzzle so jumbled it doesn't look like anything at all.

The non-puzzle puzzle is the last coherent thought I have.

Because in the next moment, I'm ripped from the van, my

hands unexpectedly meeting pavement, pebbles and debris shredding my palms. I cry out, ducking my head to protect myself from whatever is coming next.

But I'm not quick enough.

Because what comes next slams into my face with so much force that my neck snaps back and I crumple over, fading into the pavement like chalk. My ears ring, my face feels sticky, my throat burns. I try to sit up and I hear a guy groan, telling me to stay down. But I keep struggling to stand. The next hit glances off the left side of my jaw and I bite my tongue hard, rust and what I always imagined pennies would taste like filling my mouth. A swift kick to the ribs follows.

That's when everything fades to nothing.

I OPEN MY EYES SLOWLY. A bright light blinds me and I wince, the movement sending shockwaves through my brain.

A face swims in front of me before consolidating into features I don't recognize.

"Hello. My name is Dr. Kiera Lee and you're at the Georgetown University Hospital." Her voice is kind, gentle. "You've suffered a series of injuries, including facial trauma and two fractured ribs. You've received stitches above your right eye and along your lower lip. Do you know your name?"

With each blink, she grows clearer. With each blink, my eye throbs, my jaw and lips feel stiff and unmoving, and an indescribable amount of pain races throughout my body.

"Emma... Stanton," I croak, my voice low and broken. My throat raw.

"Emma, is there someone we can call for you? You came in with no identification. Do you know what happened?"

I close my eyes, recalling hazy memories. Shadowy figures. Facial hair and sunglasses. Lip Ring. "Who brought me in?"

Dr. Lee sighs. "An ambulance. A woman with young children found you lying in a park. She called 9-1-1."

A park? They beat me up in a park? Where kids play?

Oh God, a horrible thought forms and my body jerks at the possibility. "Was I... Did I..." I gasp for air, trying to form my question.

Dr. Lee touches my hand. "No. You weren't raped. Although we can still do a rape kit if you wish."

Thank God for small miracles.

"Is there someone who can come sit with you? A family member? A friend?"

No way in hell am I calling my family. My dad would lose it. I can't call Lila, Mia, or Maura for this either. They're all too far away and as much as hearing any one of their voices would calm me right now, give me a sense of peace, it would destroy them. Cassie, Gray, Luke. Those are my options.

But what the hell are their cell phone numbers? Who even learns anyone's phone number these days?

"Can you please call Barracuda on Eighth Street? It's a restaurant."

"Of course. Who should I ask to speak with?"

"Grayson Harrington," I say, my voice surprisingly steady even as tears collect in the corners of my eyes. Because as much as I want Luke to come to my bedside and pull me into a hug, mend my wounds, remind me that I'm not damaged and broken, I hurt him.

And for that reason alone, I can't bring myself to hurt him again, so I'll just keep hurting for the both of us.

"Also," Dr. Lee continues, "we found this in your pocket." She hands me a white envelope.

I nod, my fingers too stiff to properly open it.

"Would you like me to open it for you?"

I nod, dropping the envelope back in her hand.

She opens it slowly, unfolds the sheet of notebook paper, and I have to hand it to her, doesn't even glance at the writing as she holds it in front of my face.

Written there in barely legible script, I read:

Tell your boyfriend to drop out of tomorrow's fight.

29

LUKE

"Barracuda." I bite out, my mind frantic. Emma's been missing for nearly four hours and I am losing my fucking mind, desperate for some goddamn answers.

Where the hell is she? Jorge said he just ran to grab a pack of smokes. Why would she leave the restaurant open with no one here? She wouldn't. Something is wrong.

"Hello. May I please speak with Grayson Harrington?"

I know, deep in my gut, that whatever the voice on the other end of the line has to say is directly related to Emma. So I lie. "Speaking."

"Mr. Harrington, I'm so sorry to tell you this over the phone, but your friend, Emma Stanton, is a patient at The Georgetown University Hospital. She asked that we give you a call and let you –"

"What's happened to her? Is she okay? What room?" I rattle off the questions in rapid succession, my grip on the phone tightening as anger floods through me. *Why the fuck is Emma in the hospital? Who broke my beautiful girl?*

"I can't give out the specifics of Emma's injuries, but she did request us to contact you. She is in room 402."

"On my way." I hang up the phone and in three long strides I'm opening the front door.

"Hey!" Gray's voice calls out, stopping me. "Is she okay?"

"She's in the fucking hospital. Georgetown. I —"

"I'll close up and meet you there."

"Thanks." And then I'm rushing through the door, into the frigid night air, and sliding behind the wheel of my Blazer.

I don't remember the drive to the hospital.

I don't even care that I'm going to get a massive ticket for parking in the first available spot even though it's reserved for handicapped.

I don't even register the young family with the newborn baby I almost collide with as I sprint toward the elevators.

My heart is pounding and my fists are clenched tight.

Too tight.

I'm in desperate need of releasing the anger eating my stomach like a parasite. I need to find out who did this, who is responsible. I need to see my girl.

I rush into room 402 ready to demand answers, but stop short the second I'm over the threshold.

Emma's eyes swing toward mine, and I can't breathe. The fiery anger pounding through my veins turns to ice. My tightly clenched fists fall open.

My beautiful, sweet, innocent girl is lying in a hospital bed. Her eyes are soulful, filled with so many emotions that I can't get a read on any of them. Her head is bandaged. Stitches pop up in random places around her face.

"Luke."

I take two steps until I'm next to her bedside and fall to my knees. Placing my head in her lap I breathe out the emotion that is clogging my lungs, burning my eyes, stinging my nose. And I tell her the only thing that matters. The only thing I care about. Her.

"Baby, I'm so so sorry."

She laces her fingers in my hair, dragging the tips in circles. "Shh."

"You're not supposed to comfort me in this moment." I look up and let her see me. See all the feelings I have for her playing out across my face because I know that any words I use will fail to convey just how much I care about her. How much I need her. That falling in love with her is scarier than any opponent I've ever fought.

She cups the side of my face. "I'm okay."

I shake my head, anger rearing its head once more. "No, you're not. This never should have happened. Who did this? What happened?"

"How did you find me?"

"The hospital called the restaurant."

"For Gray."

"I lied and said I was him. And I don't fucking care. I don't believe that you don't want me here."

"I didn't want you to see me like this. I didn't want to hurt you any more than I already have."

"I want to see all of you. All the time. Always." My hands find hers and grip tightly, afraid she'll disappear. "I'm falling in love with you, Emma Stanton. I've been falling for you since the first day I saw you and you awkwardly tried to shake my hand."

She snorts, but her eyes blink back tears.

"I don't care why you broke up with me. I'm not letting you go. Not without a fight. And Em, we all know fights are kind of my thing."

She's openly crying now, tears tracking her cheeks. She squeezes my hands in hers, tugging me forward. I waste no time closing the distance between us and softly brush my lips over her top one.

Still, she winces and I know her mouth must be hurting. I curse under my breath. "What happened, Emma?"

"Which part?"

"What the fuck does that mean? How many parts were there?"

"I'll tell you all of it. I'll start at the beginning. But I really would love some tea first." She smiles weakly and I suddenly feel like an asshole. I never even asked her how she feels or if she needs anything. Instead, I barged into her room, unloaded my feelings on her, kissed her bruised, split lips, and demanded information.

"I'm sorry, baby." Fuck. I am apologizing a lot today. "Are you hungry? Are you tired? Do you want me to call your family?"

"No. Just tea."

"Okay then. I'll be right back." I kiss her cheek before slipping out of her room.

Walking toward the snack cart at the end of the hallway, I pass a man who catches my eye even though I can't explain why.

He's broad, in good shape, and wearing a dark hoodie. He keeps his head bent low, scrolling through something on his phone.

But as my eyes trail over him, I tag the tat on his hand. A spade, stretching along the outside of his hand, just below his pinkie finger.

My blood ices as my mind recalls the last time I saw that tattoo on a guy. And who that guy was talking to. I connect the dots.

Punching numbers into my phone, I order a tea for Emma, a coffee for myself, and a couple cookies just because. The entire time, I keep the motherfucker in my peripheral vision. He shuffles from foot to foot, bored. Every few moments, he throws a glance in my direction before looking back at his phone. He's trailing me. I'm sure of it.

Who the hell is behind this?

"Thank you." I take the hot drinks and bag of cookies from the woman and walk slowly back to Emma's room, not wanting to give away the panic that seizes my chest at this fucker being in such close proximity to my girl.

When I enter her room, I let out the breath I didn't realize I was holding that she's still safe and sound, tucked into her bed, her hospital gown hanging loosely around her shoulders. I kick the door closed behind me.

A crumpled piece of paper rests on the tray stand that I slide over her hospital bed and place the tea, coffee, and cookies on. "What's that?"

She presses the button on her hospital bed to sit up. "For you." She croaks, and I wince at the fingerprint bruises ringing her neck.

Someone is going to fucking pay.

I flip open the note. *Tell your boyfriend to drop out of tomorrow's fight.*

"Jesus." I crumple the paper in my hand and shove it into my pocket.

Emma's eyes meet mine, worry and concern lurking there. Another stab to my chest. I just want to make her happy, make her feel protected, safe. Instead, she's lying broken in a hospital bed delivering me messages that show just how much it's my fault she ended up here.

I sit next to her and take her hand in mine. "Emma, I promise I'll fix this. I'll find out who did this. I won't stop until I —"

"Don't drop out of the fight."

"What? I don't give a fuck about tomorrow's fight. I care about you and making sure you're safe. This can never happen again." I gesture to the surrounding hospital room. "Ever."

She takes a sip of her tea, nudging the cup back onto the tray when she's finished. "Don't ever give up on your dreams, Luke." A smile I don't understand flickers across her lips and when she looks at me. I'm sucker-punched by the depth of emotion in her eyes. "I'll tell you exactly what I need. I need you to chase your dreams. And then I need you to fight for me. I need to chase my dreams too and I need to fight for you. And even though this situation is so messed up and I still don't understand it all, I know that we're already doing the most important parts: the chasing and the fighting. So if you don't fight tomorrow, if you give up your dream, if you step back, then you won't be chasing after a part of life that you need. And I need you to have that so when you do fight for me, you're fighting with everything. You need to be complete, to feel whole, to be the person you want to be to have a love worth fighting for. And I want that kind of love. I want it all with you. So don't give up. Not on boxing. Not on me. Okay?"

I stare at her for several minutes, trying to absorb her words, to process the meaning behind them. "You want to be with me?"

She laughs and then winces. "Don't make me laugh. I hurt," she scolds, tracing the words that tag my knuckles. Lone Wolf. "I want to be with you. No more lone wolf. From now on, it's me and you. And we can figure out all the rest as it happens."

I inch my chair closer to her bed until I'm practically sitting in it. "You scared the shit out of me today. I can't lose you."

"You won't lose me. I won't let you." She tugs on my fingers once more and I lean over to kiss her softly, gently.

Reverently.

My sweet, innocent, beautiful girl.

"It's me plus you," I say to her, just to make sure.

She grabs my face between her bandaged hands and looks into my eyes, making sure I see what she's saying, what she's giving me. Herself.

"Me plus you."

IT'S LATE when I flip on the TV. Emma is snoring softly in her bed, her head lolled over to one side. She's beautiful. Even banged up and bandaged, she makes it difficult for me to breathe. Visiting hours ended ages ago, but I managed to sweet talk my way into staying with the night nurse. And intimated my way into staying with the security on the floor. I'm not going anywhere without her.

I flip through channels, picking up my phone to scroll through the messages I've received from Gray.

He came by earlier in the night with Cassie and the three of us huddled around Emma, offering support, and listening to her entire story as she talked to the police.

Cassie cried.

Gray looked shocked, swearing up a storm when Emma mentioned the name "Del Marco."

And I choked back my anger.

Fucking Becca.

Gray: Turn on the news.

I flip the channel.

Breaking News: Senator Preston Harrington the Third's Chief of Staff Rob Del Marco arrested this evening on

*charges of extortion and illegal gambling after a Capitol Hill
intern was injured in connection with a boxing match planned
for tomorrow night. The bout, between heavyweight champion Joe "Lightning" Carney and Senator Harrington's
nephew, contender Luke Harrington, has not been canceled
at this time. A special counsel will convene to determine if
Senator Harrington had any involvement in this ongoing
investigation.*

I throw the remote control across the room. Of course he
was involved. I knew it the second I saw the guy at the
hospital with the spade tattoo. The same tattoo as the guy
talking with Uncle P at the cafe. *Was it the same guy? Was he
one of the guys who beat Emma up? Is Uncle P letting his
Chief of Staff take the fall for him?*

I text Gray back.

Me: What's going on?

Gray: Come over.

Damn. I drop my head back in the seat. I don't want to
leave Emma alone in the hospital.

*Gray: Cassie's on her way to stay with Emma. It's
important.*

I breathe out a sigh of relief.

When Cassie walks in the room twenty minutes later, I'm
thankful to see that she brought Emma a change of clothes, a
bag of toiletries, her Kindle, and snacks. I know Emma is
special, but seeing the way my cousin, her roommate, people
she's only known for a few short months worry about her and
care for her settles some of the fear rattling around in my
chest.

"Hey. She'll be really grateful that you brought her stuff,"
I tell Cassie, nodding at the bag she's holding.

Cassie nods, her eyes trained on Emma. "Yeah. I can't
even believe any of this happened." Her voice cracks at the

end and she shakes her head, swinging her gaze to me. "I hope they catch whoever did this to her."

"They will."

"How can you sound so sure?"

"Because I am sure. You'll be okay here?"

"Yeah."

"Call me if you need anything. And keep an eye on the door. If anyone tries to come in that you don't know, call security. I'll be back as soon as I can. You have my number?"

She hands me her phone and I punch in my contact info.

"I'll see you in a bit." I watch as she pulls the chair I just vacated closer to Emma's bed and sits down.

I'm grateful Emma has friends like Cassie. Friends like Mia, Lila, and Maura. Siblings like Jon, Daphne, and Celia. Her parents. People that love her and care about her and want the best for her, just like I do. As soon as she's awake, I'm going to ask her about getting in contact with her people, letting them know what's happened so they don't worry in case her name gets leaked in conjunction with the story on the news.

Leaving Emma's room, I do a thorough search of her floor for the guy from earlier, but the hallway is quiet. I hustle out of the hospital and drive to Gray's. Punching in the security code to access the elevator, I enter his apartment.

And I trip when the face that greets me is Uncle Preston's.

"What the hell are you doing here?"

"Lucas." He's surprised to see me. "I am very sorry for what happened to Emma." His words ring with sincerity. But then again, he's a politician.

"Where's Gray?"

"Right here." Gray enters the foyer and tosses me a bottle of water. "We need to talk. All of us."

Uncle P and I follow Gray into his living room and sit down around the coffee table.

"Dad?" Gray asks.

Uncle Preston settles back against the couch cushions and pinches the bridge of his nose, a tell that he's nervous. "I knew about everything Del Marco was involved in."

Big shocker there.

"What I didn't know, and I swear this to you, Lucas, is that they would hurt Emma." He looks at me, his eyes flashing with anger. "That was a cowardly move and I would never be involved in such a thing."

"But you tried to bribe her," Gray says.

What? My eyes flash to Gray but he avoids looking at me.

"You told her that if she convinced Luke to drop the fight, you'd help her get hired on the Hill."

Uncle Preston hangs his head before looking up again. He opens his mouth to speak, but Gray continues. "And when she flat-out refused, you told her that she had to break up with him to save him from getting hurt and not squash the piece of legislation she's hung up on."

The Parental Leave issue.

Holy shit. Emma sacrificed her dream career for me?

"That's why she ended things with me? Because you told her I'd be hurt if she didn't?" I ask incredulously.

"You'll be happy to know that she didn't even consider trying to talk you out of the fight."

Of course she didn't. She's my girl. Her moral compass is as solid as gold.

"So what now?" I ask. "Why are we here?"

Gray clears his throat, looking at his dad.

"I will be canceling my plans to announce a campaign bid for the Republican nomination." Uncle P says gruffly, his eyes swinging from Gray to me. "I release you from the loan debt. And I will no longer try to push either one of you into a business or political role." His voice is quiet but steady, his Adam's apple working up and down. I can tell this is the last thing he wants to say but as Gray nods along, I get the feeling my cousin knows a lot more than he lets on.

"I'm going to pay you back anyway," I tell Uncle Preston. "If I win tomorrow, I'll cut you a check. And then we're done."

"What do you mean?"

"We're squared away with the loan. And I'm done with you. Don't come around looking for me. Don't ask about me. And don't try to talk to my girl. You and I," I point between us, "are finished. You tried to ruin the only dream I've ever had and sabotage the only relationship I've ever cared about." My breath quickens, and I feel rage taking over. "What is wrong with you? Do you hate me that much that you never want me to find happiness?"

"Lucas, please, let me explain. There's a lot you don't know and I –"

"Yeah? Like what?" I bite my tongue hard. *Why the hell am I even giving him the chance to explain?*

"The management team for Carney," he shakes his head, "there's a lot at play, various deals with the venue, things going on with the PR team, things you know nothing about."

"Dad was receiving kickbacks to help fund his campaign launch. In exchange for the kickbacks, he made promises he couldn't keep. Namely, getting you out of the fight tomorrow," Gray supplies, narrowing his eyes at his dad.

Uncle P's mouth drops open in a rare show of emotion. Gray has rendered him mute.

"The guys with the tattoos?" I ask.

"Gang members involved in the illegal gambling," Gray

scoffs. "I've spent a lot of time in the gambling world myself. Did you know that, Dad?"

Uncle P nods stiffly.

"Getting Del Marco mixed up in all of this was a mistake. He's too soft," Gray says, an edge to his voice. "He'll sing like a canary to the special counsel. You know that, right?"

Uncle P nods again.

"So basically, your time in political office is ending."

Uncle P closes his eyes, resting his head against the back of the couch.

"As is your time in this family," Gray continues, standing up and walking to the bar he has set up in the corner of his living room.

Uncle P and I both snap our necks up to stare at him.

"What are you talking about?" Uncle P asks, a sneer twisting his mouth. "Have you forgotten who funds this life-style of yours?" He gestures around Gray's opulent apartment.

"I have a job. I'll simplify. I don't want your money, especially if you're making it by getting innocent girls beaten up in parks."

"I told you, I –"

"Had nothing to do with it. I know. But your meddling has caused a lot of people a lot of heartache. And that's not something I want to be a part of or blind to, not anymore. I hope things swing in your favor with the special counsel. And I hope that one day, you and I can have the relationship I always wanted us to have. But right now," he exhales heavily, "right now, I'm with Luke. I'm done with you." He turns his back to us then and pours three fingers of Scotch neat. "Would anyone like a drink?"

I watch Uncle P's face crumble. While the reaction playing out on his face is genuine, it's still too little, too late.

30

LUKE

I sit by Emma's side the entire night.

Her phone buzzes all night long with messages from family and friends checking up on her. I had to talk her into calling them all, but in the end, even she agreed that it was better they hear what happened from her than from the news. At 6:00 AM, I answer an incoming call from her dad.

"Hello? Mr. Stanton? It's Luke."

"Luke? Hi, how are you? I know that you're staying with Emmy. How is she?" His voice is laced with worry and gruff with exhaustion. "How is she really? I know what she told her mother, but I can be there in two hours."

I nod in understanding. If I wasn't with Emma right now, I'd walk to see her. "I understand your concern, sir. Truthfully, she's sleeping. A lot. She looks roughed up, physically speaking. But emotionally and mentally, she's herself. Asked me to bring her a cupcake with a side of ice cream for dinner."

"That sounds like her. Listen, I know Emma's going to your fight later today but, would you mind if I joined? I just need to see her for myself. Her mother and I are sick with worry and – "

"I'd really like to meet you, Mr. Stanton. I'll arrange for you and Emma to sit ringside. She's insisting on coming to the fight, even though I think she should be resting. To be honest, it would make me feel better if she was with family."

"Thank you, Luke. Thank you for being there and for taking care of her. You have no idea how much it means to a dad to know his little girl is in good hands."

"It's not a problem."

"Okay then, I look forward to meeting you later today. Good luck tonight."

Mr. Stanton hangs up, and I collapse back in my chair. Jesus. I've never been the type of guy a girl brings around to meet her parents. Unless she was in some reckless stage and desperately wanted to piss them off. I'm positive that every dad who's taken one look at me automatically thanks God that his daughter isn't dating me or, if she is, prays that she kicks me to the curb real fast.

I shake my head and rub the sleep from my eyes. Sleeping sitting up in a chair doesn't provide the best rest, especially before the fight that will set the trajectory of my professional career. But it doesn't matter. None of it does. Only her.

THE LOCKER ROOM IS SILENT.

Completely quiet.

So still I can hear my breath working its way through my lungs and out of my mouth. This is it. The moment I've trained for, sweated for, pushed myself to the physical and mental limits for. The moment I've dreamed of, thought about, ran through my mind on a running loop.

How would it feel? Would I be sick with nerves? Pumped with adrenaline? Excited to accept the challenge?

Now that it's here, I'm holding onto mixed feelings. Nerves for sure. Adrenaline, my old friend, is in attendance. Excited? Fuck yeah. But I'm also angry. My beautiful girl is sitting ringside, against my advice, against my wishes. Still, she's here. And now every time I look over at her tonight, I'll remember who I'm fighting for.

Emma.

The girl who reminded me to chase my dreams.

To fight for what I want.

The girl who risked it all so I could walk out into a venue filled with thousands of people and have my shot at a title.

A fucking title.

When the only title I care about right now is boyfriend.

I laugh at myself, walk over to the sink, and stare at my reflection in the mirror. It's not cracked or chipped. I've come a long, long way in a short amount of time. Which just means the fall is greater. And there's no way I'm surrendering tonight to anyone.

Especially not to Lightning.

Tonight, I'm going to be a champion.

"It's time," Ammo calls out from the door.

I brace my hands against the sides of the sink and nod at myself.

I can do this. I have to do this.

I will do this.

So yeah, I'm nervous, excited, angry, all of it.

But when I step out of the locker room door and hear the chants and cheers, see the bright lights and insane crowd of people, breathe in the moment, I'm just relieved that I made it here at all.

I CAN FEEL her eyes on me as I step into the ring.

It's crazy, really. There are thousands of people here and I swear, even if I didn't know exactly where she's sitting, I'd be able to feel her stare. She's here, and that's all that matters.

I take a seat in my corner and Scoop nods at me, hunching down on the balls of his feet to look me in the eyes and make sure my head is on straight. It is. I know what I'm here for, and I'm not leaving without a win.

"You ready?"

"Yes."

"He's going to push you, challenge you, maybe even talk a bunch of shit. Keep your head clear, stay focused, do what we've been doing every day in the gym, and this is yours. Be first, every single jab, each combo, be first. Hear me?"

"I hear you."

The referee motions us forward and the guy shadowing me to make sure my wrapped hands stay wrapped without any tampering steps back. Lightning and I come face to face and for just a second, I'm star struck. Imagine standing across from someone you idolized, worshipped, cheered for, for most of your adolescence. Got that feeling of awe mixed with excitement? Now pretend you have to punch them in the face. It's a strange moment for me.

The ref runs through the rules. Lightning and I nod at each other, tapping gloves.

The bell sounds.

Round One begins.

HE'S FAST. Faster than I thought he'd be. Fast like Ammo.

It's the ninth round.

My breath leaves my lips in hesitant puffs, and I'm winded.

One, two, hook.

He catches my left cheek, his glove glancing off my jaw. Another punch to my right side. I stumble backward, knowing if he gets me in the corner against the ropes, it's all over.

Keep moving. Stay starving.

I turn at the last minute, getting my back to the wide space of the ring.

Jab, jab, cross.

I get one hit in and Lightning sneers, a drop of blood glistening in the corner of his mouth.

I punch again, landing it solidly. Again. Again. A combination that catches him off guard.

I'm pushing him back, jamming him up in the corner.

Against the ropes.

One, two, three, four hits.

His arms come up to frame his face, to protect himself.

I unleash all the fury coursing through my veins. The anger over my dad's death, Uncle Steve's passing, Uncle P's meddling. The blinding rage over what happened to Emma, over almost losing her. I stop thinking; my mind shuts down completely. It's just the sound of my ragged breathing, the overwhelming swell of emotions, and the pure physicality of doing what I love. This moment stretches into an eternity when in reality it's only seconds.

And then, the bell.

The referee calling a technical knockout.

Raising my right arm.

I won.

A stunned silence washes over the crowd. A fringe

contender, a nobody, stepping up to beat Joe "Lightning" Carney in a title fight was unthinkable... until thirty seconds ago.

Then the crowd goes wild. Cheering and screaming and a flash of colors, a vibe of energy that pulses throughout the entire venue.

I find her face in the crowd. She's standing, clapping, cheering, pure sunshine streaming from her beautiful smile. Her dad stands next to her, his arms raised above his head as he cheers for me.

I can't stop the huge grin that splits my face.

Finally, a moment I can be proud of.

31

EMMA

"Emma? Can you come in for a second?" LeBeau's voice floats out of his office door to where I am currently standing next to the coffee pot.

"Sure. Want a coffee?" I offer, adding cream and sugar to the mug I just poured for myself. I take a tentative sip, wincing as the hot liquid stings the cuts along my lips and the inside of my mouth. Still, I need caffeine. The recurring nightmares that have been keeping me awake make for very long days.

"No thanks."

I step inside LeBeau's office with my mug and take a seat across from him. In a way, things have changed so rapidly since everything went down outside Barracuda. It's only been a week but in that time, I've changed. I've gained a newfound confidence, a fresh perspective on my life and the future I want to pursue. I've had the privilege of watching Luke win his title, claim a championship belt. I can't even describe the pride I felt witnessing such a significant moment for him. I bravely told him exactly how I felt and, even after laying it all on the line, he wants to be with me. We're now an "us" and that alone has me reshuffling my priorities.

Sporting my new look as bruised and broken, I've stopped trying to be or look perfect for anyone and am more concerned with enjoying each new day, learning something new, and employing the type of self-care I deserve that's been lacking for way too long. Which is why, even though I'm incredibly eager to hear whatever LeBeau has to say, I also am focused on drinking my beverage while it's still hot.

"How are you?"

"I'm doing pretty good, thanks. How are you?" The weird thing is, it's the truth. I *am* doing pretty good. Even though I look like a bruised-up mess and am exhausted from the nightmares, my heart feels light and filled up with all the feels. I know Luke has a lot to do with that. Besides supporting me to chase my dreams, he's fighting my nightmares by my side. Drawing from his strength and steadiness, each night gets easier and each day brighter.

"Fine, thanks."

Silence ensues, and even though it could be awkward, I'm too tired to pay it much attention.

"Well," Senator LeBeau clears his throat, "I wanted to discuss your post-graduation plans."

I sit up straighter in my chair. This is the moment I've worked toward for the entire semester. This has been my focus for the past four months. All the reading and research and coffee runs have come down to this moment where LeBeau will decide if I begin my career on Capitol Hill or not.

"I know that you were hoping to secure employment here for after graduation, but I'm sorry to tell you that isn't going to be possible." He shakes his head, regret shadowing his expression.

A twinge of sadness pierces my heart as I process his words. Even though a part of me, the piece still hanging onto the Emma who descended on DC with a masterplan and a life goal, is incredibly disappointed, another part of me knows I can seek out a new opportunity. Keeping my face smooth, I nod again. "I understand. Thank you very much for the opportunity to intern in your office. I've learned a lot and the experience here has been invaluable."

"I'm glad to hear that. I really wish there was more I could do, but our budget for next year is even less than it was this year." He shakes his head again. "After everything that happened with your dad I..." he pauses, his thumb clicking the back of a pen, "I was hoping I'd at least be able to help you out more. I had no idea that investment would go south so quickly."

Say what? This has my neck snapping up, my eyes flashing to LeBeau's. "The investment?"

LeBeau nods, dropping his pen and laying his palm flat against his desk. "It was supposed to be a sure thing. I had no idea when I discussed it with Gerald that things would take such a nosedive. Nor did I know the amount of money he had sunk into it. Had I known the full story; I would have advised him differently." He shrugs, as if the whole thing is just water under the bridge now. As if my childhood home isn't currently on the market to be sold. As if my mom wasn't struggling to reenter a workforce so drastically different from the one she left over twenty years ago.

I make a noncommittal sound in my throat, scared that if I open my mouth all the wrong things will come pouring out.

LeBeau sighs. "Of course, if you need any recommendations during your job search, I would be happy to provide you with one. I'm sure you'll have no problem finding a job here,

Emma. You're bright, dedicated, and extremely motivated. You'll be fine."

In a matter of blinks, my perception of LeBeau morphs from a public servant proudly serving his country to one of a common politician, complete with smooth lines and fake smiles. I stare at him, confused.

This was my dream! To sit in an office like this and work on issues that matter to Americans, to people, to families. To improve the standard of living and the quality of life here. To do something that matters. In this moment, the whole promise of that has popped like a balloon and I'm left feeling deflated, empty, drained.

"What's happening with the Parental Leave bill?"

"That's on hold for now. Immigration Reform and the new healthcare bill are more important at this time. But I really appreciate all the research you've done on the issue."

I nod, a sharp pain stabbing me in the chest as I realize my aspirational future is dead. "That's good. Thank you again for the opportunity."

Walking out of LeBeau's office for the last time, I pose for pictures with the other staff members, shake hands with Jenn and Zoe, and even share a quick hug goodbye with Courtney. I wrap up my last day amid smiles, laughter, and a feeling of general geniality.

No, the irony is not lost on me. It took me until the last moment of my internship, until my final days in DC, to master my poker face, but I think I pulled it off quite successfully.

I have to share the news with Gray.

———

"CAN YOU EVEN BELIEVE THAT?" I whine across the bar from

Gray where I'm plopped on a barstool drinking my signature Diet Coke. "He was just so dismissive. As if this isn't my future on the line. As if he didn't somehow influence my dad's financial downfall. Ugh, politics." I squeeze extra lemon into my glass and give a swirl with my straw.

"You're overthinking it, babe." Luke saunters up behind me, bending to kiss me. "Politicians are politicians. Your expectations are too high. Just look at Uncle P."

Gray shakes his head behind the bar, leaning forward so his forearms rest on the ledge. "Come on, Stanton, you're better than this."

"Then what?" I ask miserably, still swirling my Diet Coke, my future dreams of working on The Hill squashed.

"Then thinking that one or two or even fifty politicians define what you do. The guys like LeBeau, like my dad, they don't really matter. That's the problem with this town. This is why I have no desire to enter politics and have pushed back against my dad on the issue."

"Why?" Luke and I ask in unison.

"Because while what they do is extremely important and keeps things moving in our country, it's too polarized. I mean, have you ever heard of any other democracy with only two political parties that wield all the power? Everything is either 'right' or 'left', 'red' or 'blue'." He uses air quotes and I smirk, even though listening to Gray wax on about the U.S. political system is something I never expected to hear. "I like to think that all civil servants start out with the belief of making the country, the world, whatever, a better place." He juts his jaw in my direction. "Kind of like you. And then somewhere along the way, they get caught up in the system. In order to win in the system, you have to play by the rules already laid out. There are two parties, and you have to align with one of them. As time goes on, maybe you even have to become more extreme in the views you propose in order to get the votes. As time passes, you grow farther and farther away from the bright-eyed, sincere girl or guy who started out wanting to make things better. You forget what matters."

"Which is?" Luke asks, his tone bored.

"Ideas, beliefs, and a willingness to stand by the principles you value. Are you willing to act for things like injustice? Are you willing to do the right thing even when it may hurt your own success because it's unpopular?" He raises his eyebrows at me. "What matters are the things that hold you together: family, faith, love, passion. Those things don't fit neatly into one political party, they never have. So, Stanton, look around. You're in the capital of the U.S. You don't have to be on Capitol Hill to do good for others. You don't have to work for a Senator or Congressman to work on the issues you care about. You don't have to make yourself neatly fit into one box when there are tons of other opportunities you can pursue here. Make sense?"

I stare at him in awe. I think Luke is shocked into silence. Who knew I would get schooled by Gray at the end of my internship? First, the guy teaches me about poker faces. Now, he tells me exactly how I can be fulfilled and pursue a dream I thought was dead only moments before.

"You're right. Wow, Gray, you're really right."

"I'm always right. You should know this by now." He fixes me with a look. "You too." He glares at Luke, who still hasn't said anything. "Well, now that I've just dropped some knowledge on you guys, I'm going to swing by the coffee house down the street and hit on the pretty barista. I'm planning to take her out this weekend." He concludes, tossing down a bar towel and strolling out of the restaurant without a backward glance.

Luke and I turn toward each other, a beat of silence passing, before we crack up. Well, I crack up, laughter erupting out of me in spurts as I hunch over and grab my stomach. Luke lets out a chuckle bordering on a small laugh. Progress.

Leave it to Gray to make the entire day better.

Luke presses a kiss against the side of my neck.

Leave it to Luke to make every day the best.

Tossing another pile of sweaters in the open suitcase on the floor, I watch Emma in the mirror as she packs up the pencil skirts and blazers hanging in her closet. God, I'm going to miss this girl. My girl. If someone told me four months ago that I would have been this twisted up about a girl, that I would be helping her move, that I would be devastated about it, I would have laughed until I cracked a rib.

Yet here I am.

"Do you think I should keep this?" she holds up a black jacket.

"Looks nice."

She rolls her eyes and laughs. "It's kind of worn looking." She tosses it into a pile she deemed "donate." And isn't that awesome? That she donates the clothes she doesn't want any more to help others instead of trying to sell them at a consignment shop or just stuffing them in a trash bag like I do.

"Em," I lock eyes with her in the mirror and watch as a smile spreads across her lips. "I'm going to miss you."

"Me too." She walks toward me, sitting down cross-legged on the other side of the suitcase so that she's facing me over the piles of her clothes. "But I'll be moving here in June! Can you believe it?"

Of course I believe it. I never doubted Emma would land her dream job, even if it wasn't her original dream. After talking to Gray, she reached out to several NGO's and non-profits. Within a week, she had three interviews lined up to work on women's issues, particularly women's health issues. Just yesterday, she received an offer letter for after graduation. I couldn't be prouder of her. "DC, your new team at work, me," I shake my head, "we're all going to be extremely lucky the day you move here on a permanent basis."

"I still can't believe I'm leaving here with a job. It's like fate, you know?"

"Nah, it's called hard work and perseverance, Emma. You never gave up. I'm proud of you, babe."

"Thanks, Luke. And I'm super proud of you! Paying back your uncle, planning to renovate Barracuda, training under Scoop," she bites her bottom lip, "it's all falling into place for you."

"For us."

"For us," she repeats. "I've been meaning to ask you something."

Uh-oh. I've yet to hear a girl say those words and not have the conversation end in a blaze of tears. Her tears. "Shoot."

She fidgets with the zipper on the suitcase as she meets my gaze. Her blue eyes are so deep I could swim in them. "I know you're going to be really busy over the holidays, with the renovations and all, but my best friends and I –"

"Mia, Lila, and Maura?"

"Yes. The four of us are meeting up in New York City on January 7. Cade arranged the whole thing as a Christmas present to Lila. She doesn't even know yet."

"The football player and the blonde in LA?"

"Correct. We're meeting at a restaurant in the city and then going for a night out."

"That's cool."

"Will you come with me?"

"Of course."

"And then stay for a few days to meet the rest of my family?" She adds. "Everyone is super jealous that Dad met you. He keeps going on and on about how I'm dating the next Floyd Mayweather and now everyone, and I mean *everyone*, is curious."

"Your dad is really cool. Not like any dad I've ever met," I tell her honestly, recalling our first interaction. The way he kept pumping my hand up and down and thanking me for taking care of Emma. How his eyes raked over my tattoos and instead of judging them, he asked questions, wanting to know more about them, about me. I've never met a dad like that before. Mr. Stanton is one in a million.

"Don't tell him that. And please, don't let anyone in my family force you to autograph anything. Especially my little cousins."

I give her a look.

"I'm serious."

"Okay."

"Just a warning, my friends are going to love you, maybe even more than my family."

"If you say so. But I'll be there. I'll drive up the first week of January."

Her eyes dance with excitement and her whole face lights up. "It's going to be the best."

"Any time spent with you is the best."

"Ha! You're picking up lines from Gray."

I chuckle.

"Anyway, since I won't see you for Christmas, I wanted to give you your present now."

"You didn't have to get me anything, babe. Just getting to be with you is more than enough. And knowing that you're moving here in June, that's enough Christmas gifts to last a lifetime."

She rolls her eyes.

I bite the inside of my cheek to keep from smiling. Man, I've never smiled so much in my life until Emma Stanton turned my world upside down.

"I have something to show you too."

"For Christmas?"

"For whatever."

"Okay. But me first." She scoots closer, pushing the suitcase out of the way. Placing her hands over my eyes she says, "Close your eyes. No peeking."

I do as she says, sitting on her bedroom floor with my eyes closed, waiting for a Christmas present like a little kid. The guys at the gym would knock me out if they could see me like this. But it's worth it if it makes Em happy.

"Okay. Open them."

I open my eyes and suck in a breath.

Standing before me in a pair of deep purple panties, Emma looks as radiant as the freaking sun. Jesus, I could stare at her for forever and it still wouldn't be enough. "You're perfect." I lean forward onto my knees and reach out to touch the smooth silk of her creamy skin.

"You're not paying attention. Look closer." She angles her body to the left.

I swallow thickly, my eyes finally noticing what she's talking about.

There, in black script, right under the soft swell of her left breast, are my initials followed by a plus sign followed by her initials: LH + ES. Two hearts follow the S, shaded in with a soft pink.

"Merry Christmas." She says as my eyes snap up to hers. "Do you like it?" She sounds unsure and I jump to my feet to take away any doubt she feels for permanently marking her body for me, for us.

A snort of laughter shoots out of me as I reach behind my neck and tug off my shirt. Emma's eyes widen as I show her the inside of my right arm. In a thin, free-flowing font, "Emma" marks the inside of my bicep, stretching from the crease in my elbow to just below my armpit. The skin around the tattoo is still red as it heals.

"You didn't?"

"I want you, Emma Stanton. For always. It's me plus you." I step over her suitcase to where she's standing and pull her into my arms, laying kisses across every inch of her skin.

She laughs, pressing her lips into the side of my neck.

I walk her backwards to where her bed waits, the back of her knees hitting the mattress as I fall over her, the crumpled sheets a happy reminder of our morning together. Laying her down beneath me, I can't help but stare down at her and take in all her beautiful perfection.

"Me plus you," I tell her again, capturing her lips in a sweet kiss.

"Me plus you."

That's the last thing she says because what follows is a very hot, extremely sexy, somewhat sweaty, bout beneath her sheets.

JANUARY

EMMA

M y feet practically skim the tops of the sidewalk with how quickly I'm walking. "Hurry up." I tug on Luke's hand, pulling him behind me.

"We have plenty of time, babe."

"Cade said 7:00 PM. I bet the girls are already there. I can't wait to see them!"

"I know."

Grinning, I wrap my arms around his, hugging him against me. "I'm so happy you're here. So excited for you to meet my friends."

"Me too, babe."

Two blocks later, I see the sign for Marco's Ristorante. Looking closer, I spot Mia and Maura huddled together in front of the restaurant, two guys flanking their sides. I recognize Zach Huntington immediately. And the other guy is most definitely Mia's Italiano. "Hello!" I call out, running toward them.

They both look up and giant smiles form on their faces when they see me.

"You're here!" Mia shrieks, walking toward me.

"Finally." Maura adds. "Now we're just waiting on the California girl."

I throw my arms around my friends, pulling them into me and dropping my forehead onto their shoulders. "I've missed you guys."

Mia hugs me back fiercely while Maura pats my back, trying to avoid the affectionate embrace. I hug her closer. We break apart, the three of us about to speak at the same time when Lila's shriek of pure delight cuts through the air.

Turning around, I see her sprinting down the sidewalk to meet us. She sails through the air, practically knocking me over with the force of her body as she plows into our little group. I catch a glimpse of Luke over her shoulder, chuckling into his fist as he watches us.

"This is the best day ever!" Lila yells, looking at the insanely hot guy shadowing her.

"He did a great job planning the whole thing," Mia adds, smiling at Cade.

Lila turns back toward us and throws her arms as wide as they go. We all huddle in for another hug. "I can't believe you're all here."

"I can't believe you're all this much into hugging," Maura muffles into my shoulder.

"I have so much to tell you guys," I admit.

"Me too," Mia adds. "So much."

"Let's never spend this much time apart again," Lila demands. "It was too long."

I nod, my head bumping with Mia's. We laugh.

"I feel like so much has happened," I whine.

"Because it has," Maura says rationally, reaching up to tug her hat lower on her head. "It's freezing out."

"I know. I forgot how lame winter is." Lila rolls her eyes,

flipping her blonde wavy hair over her shoulder. "Come on, let's go inside. I hear the food is delicious here."

We all turn, keeping our arms linked for warmth as we shuffle the last few steps to the door of Marco's. Immediately, we're all trying to talk at once.

"Uh, girls?" A guy's voice calls out from behind us.

Turning around, I laugh as I see Luke standing with the guys my best friends have chosen as theirs. Four incredibly hot, amazingly sweet, sincere men watching us with a mixture of amusement and curiosity.

Maura snorts. "I guess we all did pretty good upholding the pact."

Mia smiles sweetly. "Definitely."

I nod in agreement.

Lila huffs, "Well, are you guys coming or what?"

Cade shakes his head, Lorenzo barks out a laugh, Zach nods, and Luke's eyes meet mine with an intensity I never want to lose. Surrounded by my best friends and the guys we love, the guys who chose us back, I can't even wait to see where the Spring semester will take us all. And I'm really, really grateful to experience it with the people I love best by my side.

FIVE YEARS LATER

EPILOGUE

LUKE

"Luke?"

"In the kitchen, babe."

She turns the corner and enters the kitchen, her lips curved in a smile, her eyes dancing.

"What's going on?" I ask, passing her a wine glass as she toes off her heels.

"Oh my God." She squeals, standing on her tippy toes to sweep a kiss over my mouth. "The most amazing thing happened."

"Tell me." I sweep her hair to one side and grip the back of her neck, dropping a kiss to the sweet spot beneath her ear.

"Wait! Don't distract me." Emma laughs, leading me back to the kitchen island where she hops onto a barstool and takes a sip of wine.

"Tell me quickly then."

"The Parental Leave bill just passed! In the House and the Senate!"

"Oh wow, babe, that's incredible." I slip my hands underneath her thighs and lift her onto the countertop, stepping in between her thighs.

"I know! I can hardly believe it." She twists her arms around my neck and pulls me in for a hard kiss. "I feel like I've been working on this for forever."

"Five years is a long time."

"Lobbying is so hard sometimes."

"But you love it."

"But I love it." She bites her lower lip, her eyes sparkling.

"I love you." I whisper, dropping my mouth to the shell of her ear. "And I'm so fucking proud of you."

"Love you more, Luke." She tugs me closer as I lay her out on the kitchen island.

Folding over her, I kiss her recklessly, my fingers digging in her hair as she moans into my mouth. Five years together, and I still can't get enough of her.

Pulling back, I slowly undo the buttons lining her shirt, disappearing into the waistband of her skirt. My girl, always so proper in public, is a completely different person in the bedroom. Or kitchen.

Her eyelids grow heavy, her breathing accelerating as I push her shirt off her shoulders, my eyes drinking her in, my hands palming her breasts.

"When's training start?" she asks as I dip my mouth to her belly button, making her giggle.

"Two more weeks."

"So we have time."

I tug her skirt over her hips and drop it to the floor.

"Baby, we have all the time in the world." I cover her body with mine as we christen our new kitchen island.

"OH WOW, LUKE THIS IS AMAZING." Emma scoops a second helping of pasta to her plate.

"You think so? I tried something new."

"You turned out to be quite the cook."

"Well, I do have a few restaurants, you know."

Emma snorts. "Yeah. How's Gray managing the expansion?"

"He's doing great. You know Gray, he's so easygoing about everything. But the third location is growing quickly."

"I'm impressed."

"You and me both." I take a swig of my Corona.

"I can't believe it's our first night in our new home." Emma says, looking around our beautiful kitchen complete with quartz countertops, custom cabinets, and top-of-the-line stainless steel appliances. "Thank you for everything, Luke."

"Babe, we built our home together."

"Yeah, but —"

"A house is just a house. The people inside it make it a home."

"I know, but —"

"You're my home, babe. For always."

"Promise?"

"Promise." I lean over and capture my girl's lips.

It's a promise I intend to keep forever.

THANK you so much for reading! I hope you loved the suspense underlining Emma and Luke's romance!

Make sure you catch up with Mia in *Kiss Me Goodnight in Rome* to read all about her hot-fling-turned-more with Italian race car driver, Lorenzo Barca.